My name is Callum Ormond.
I was a hunted fugitive.
My story continues . . .

CONSPIRACY 365

REVENGE

To Libby

First American Edition 2012
Kane Miller, A Division of EDC Publishing

Text copyright © Gabrielle Lord, 2011
Co-written by Rebecca Young
Cover design copyright © Scholastic Australia, 2011
Cover design and internal graphics by Nicole Leary
Cover logo designed by Natalie Winter

First published by Scholastic Australia Pty Limited in 2011.
This edition published under license from Scholastic Australia Pty Limited.

Library of Congress Control Number: 2011933990

Printed and bound in the United States of America
1 2 3 4 5 6 7 8 9 10
ISBN: 978-1-61067-082-1

CONSPIRACY 365

REVENGE

GABRIELLE LORD

Kane Miller

A DIVISION OF EDC PUBLISHING

Prologue

I knew something was wrong as soon as I saw the envelope.

It was waiting for me on my pillow. A red wax seal marked it like a thick, wet drop of blood.

I ran to the window and looked out, but the front yard was dark and quiet. Cautiously, I pulled the curtains back across and picked up the creamy-colored envelope.

The front was blank, but the seal on the back was carefully pressed with something feathered. I held it under my lamp.

A chill shuddered through my body.

I tore open the envelope and stared at the cryptic message stamped on the note inside.

For a split second I thought it was a hoax—something one of those relentless journalists, like Ben Willoughby, had snuck into my room in a desperate attempt to force another story out of me.

Some people thought that "Callum Ormond, the Teen Fugitive," was more interesting as a monster. They were always trying to poke and prod me, trying to tempt the "Psycho Kid" out of his slumber. All for another photo and another headline.

And when they finally accepted that I wasn't a crazed maniac, it was almost like they were disappointed.

But this didn't look like a journalist's prank. The tattered wings on the seal . . . and the way the ink was stamped so firmly on the note inside . . . this was different.

Something Winter had warned me about since we left Ireland kept replaying in my head. The thought sent a shock wave through my body and awoke a feeling that I'd only so recently put to rest.

Fear.

I shoved the note into my pocket, telling myself over and over again that it was nothing.

Just a hoax. Some idiot's idea of a joke.

I took one last look out the window into the empty darkness, then headed downstairs.

We were having a movie night to kick off school vacation. Mum and Gab were already in bed, and Boges, Winter and Ryan were coming over to watch a midnight horror movie in our home theater.

I had popcorn and ice cream ready, and a shiny new copy of *Nosferatu*—"the original vampire movie," so Ryan had said. Turns out he's a huge horror fan. I tore the plastic off the DVD case as I sat back in one of the eight brand-new recliners.

I stared into the hollow eyes of the ghoulish figure on the cover. He wore a long black coat, claws poised for trouble.

Was trouble coming to find me again?

Since being back home with Mum and Gab, I'd wanted everything to be perfect for us. Claiming the Ormond Singularity meant that we had more money than we knew what to do with, but after living alone in storm water drains, the bush, derelict houses, under bridges . . . I just wanted us to be together.

I'd spent a bit of money on spoiling Gab. I'd taken her out shopping, thrown her a huge surprise slumber party (with Mum's help), and given her a silver bracelet with a tiny crown charm—since she now liked to think of herself as royalty.

I also had our old rumpus room converted into the home theater, like the one in that Dolphin Point mansion I'd hidden in for a while (only in this one I didn't need to sneak around like my life depended on it).

Free stuff was always turning up on our doorstep, too. Companies would send me sneakers, backpacks, hoodies, cell phones, skateboards, even helicopter lessons—they all wanted the famous Cal Ormond to endorse their products. They'd sent Mum and Gab a few things too: jewelry, books, kitchen stuff . . . they'd even been invited on the first voyage of the *Sapphire Star*— the largest luxury cruise ship in the world. Mum and Gab couldn't wait to visit the exotic islands on the itinerary.

My friends were running late. I leaned back in my chair and held my hand up in the projector light. I was scraping the shadow of a claw across the wall when I heard a car pull up out front.

I jumped up, jogged to the door and opened it, expecting to find Ryan's car in the driveway.

But it wasn't him.

Instead, I spotted the humming silhouette of a dark car without its headlights on, idling by the curb. I ducked back inside, out of sight, waiting for the blinding flash of a long-lens camera.

But it didn't come.

Slowly, I peered out again. The car was still sitting there.

In only a few months, stacks of books had been written about me. There were thousands of blog posts and YouTube clips about my life on the run, and my Facebook page had been invaded by fans and freaks. Complete strangers followed me and called out my name wherever I went. I'd spent 365 days on the run from cops and criminals, disguising my looks, hiding in the shadows, trying to survive . . . and yet after claiming the Ormond Singularity, proving my innocence and returning home, I was ducking for cover at every corner with almost as much vigilance. When was it going to end?

Still rattled from the note left on my pillow, my fear quickly morphed into anger. I stared at the car, rage surging through me.

"What do you want?" I shouted, storming out of the house. "Haven't you seen enough of me already? How could you want *more* photos of me? You want to see me angry? Here I am!"

The car didn't move.

I stepped forward.

"Is that you, Willoughby?" I shouted. "Did you break in and plant that stupid note?" I pulled it out of my pocket and waved it. "Leave me and my family alone! And get away from my property!"

The car accelerated, screeching away.

"That's right, get out of here!" I added, before stumbling, as a sharp pain pierced my right thigh.

Shoot, I thought to myself. I must have brushed against Mum's new rose bush.

The vehicle disappeared, and I stood back up and scanned the street, waiting for nearby verandah lights to come on, followed by my weary-eyed neighbors, frustrated that Cal Ormond had brought unwanted attention to Flood Street once more.

But no lights came on. Nothing stirred.

The smell of burnt rubber drifted across the lawn as I stumbled again, falling to my hands and knees. The pain in my thigh throbbed. This was no rose thorn.

Something, someone had . . .

My chest tightened. I struggled for breath.

Gotta get help.

Under the streetlight, my vision blurring, I tried to focus on the note . . .

30 DAYS

DAY 1

30 days to go . . .

Cal's House
Flood Street, Richmond

12:11 am

"Cal?" I whispered, from outside the front door. "Dude, we're all here. Come on, let us in!"

"It's only just after midnight, right?" asked Winter. "We're not that late. What's he doing?"

"I bet he's fallen asleep, front row center," said Ryan, pulling out his phone to call Cal.

"Warm enough?" I scoffed, smirking at Winter's thick black coat and wool scarf wrapped firmly around her neck. She had wound her long, dark hair into two loose buns sitting just over her ears, making it look like she was wearing fuzzy earmuffs.

"Shh!" Winter held her hand up at me with an annoying flick before lifting a bun and pressing her ear to the door.

"It's ringing," said Ryan, turning his phone to

face us. A picture he took of Cal at a backyard barbecue the other day flashed on the screen.

"Come on, Cal, wake up," she sang softly, willing him to come to the door. "It's chilly out here."

But the phone kept on ringing.

"Cal!" I whispered louder, trying to project my voice towards the theater room.

"Boges, you're going to wake up the others," Winter hissed back, before snatching at a bag of chips that was poking out of Ryan's backpack. "Ryan, ring him again, will you?"

Ryan shrugged, clearly not as annoyed as I was at being bossed around by Winter Frey. What is it about that girl that lets her get away with it? I shook my head at Ryan. You and Cal are two peas in a pod, I thought to myself.

The three of us huddled by the door as Ryan tried Cal's phone again.

"Maddy coming tonight?" Winter asked. She kept her arms tightly folded as she bumped me with her hip. "How's it all going? You looking after her? Treating her right?"

I pretended to tip my hat. "Miss Frey, I am nothing but a gentleman," I said, in what I thought was a pretty posh English accent. "Seriously though, Mad's awesome. She has a triathlon at the crack of dawn tomorrow, so she had to have an early one tonight. We've been out a couple of times . . . and jogging together after school."

"I thought you were looking good," she said, nodding playfully. "Ready to take on NASA's robotics team?"

"Think so," I replied.

I'd been lucky enough to swing an interview with NASA's recruitment guys, even though I hadn't finished school yet, and I was hoping my grades and growing list of robotic creations would help me score the rare internship on offer. It would be a dream come true.

"Yeah, dude, show us your guns," added Ryan, phone to his ear. "Make sure you whip them out in the interview," he joked. "Pretty impressive."

I flexed my biceps, but dropped my arms when Ryan looked at his phone and shook his head.

"It's just ringing out," he said. "Maybe we should do this movie thing tomorrow night instead." Ryan yawned and tossed his car keys up and down. "Cal was pummeled at our surf session today. He's probably dead to the world. I'm going to head home, anyone want a ride?"

Winter paused before taking up his offer. "Sure," she said softly. She looked at me. "You coming with us?"

"I'm all right," I said. "I'll walk home. But I'll take those," I added, snatching the bag of chips from Winter before heading out to the street.

She chased after me and tugged on the back of my shirt. "See you back here tomorrow night?"

"Sure thing."

Home
Dorothy Road, Richmond

10:32 am

📱 dude, what happened last night? midnight too late for u these days? keen for movie tonight instead? ryan & winter r in.

12:20 pm

📱 cal, what's the deal? surely you're up by now. call me.

6:05 pm

The phone started ringing as soon as I sat down at my desk to catch up on some reading. I sighed and reached for my cell.

I groaned when I saw Winter's name come up on my screen.

"No offense," I said, "but I was kinda hoping you'd be Cal."

Winter exhaled loudly. "So you haven't heard from him either?"

"Nope. Been trying him all day."

"He was supposed to meet me at my place this morning, but he never showed. I've called him about ten times—no answer. It's weird. I think I might just go over and see him now. Want to meet me there?"

"Um—" I hesitated. Lately I'd been completely distracted by my latest surveillance designs and robotic inventions. My floor was covered with sketches and wires and microchips. I cringed at my textbooks, sitting in a stack, practically unopened for days. They could wait one more day. "Yep, I'll come, too," I finally answered. "Maybe Cal's phone battery's dead, and he's just forgotten to charge it."

"Maybe. Meet you over there at, hang on—" Winter paused. "Is seven OK?"

"Sure, see you there."

I spun around in my chair and stared into my new freshwater fish tank. It was something my uncle and I had built together a few weekends ago. It was eight feet wide and took up the length of an entire wall.

I had two archerfish in there, one slightly bigger than the other, and they were both eyeing a tiny green bug that was making its way along a thin, overhanging branch. I froze as the fish lined up the target and stealthily glided their snouts towards the water's surface. I'd been waiting to witness this moment for ages, and now not only was one archer aiming up, but two!

Out of the bigger archer's mouth shot a powerful jet of water, directly connecting with the bug! Caught in the spray, the bug turned and tumbled down into the water below. In a split second, the smaller archer had flipped its tail and snapped the stolen prey into its jaws. The bigger archer was strong, but the smaller one was fast.

And the bug was gone. Just like that.

Cal's House
Flood Street, Richmond

7:01 pm

"Boges, come in, come in," said Mrs. Ormond, waving me inside and towards the kitchen. The smell of lasagna and garlic bread filled the air, and my stomach grumbled.

"Thanks, Mrs. O.—smells delicious, as always."

"Cal's not here, you know," came a voice from behind me.

"Gab!"

"Boges!" she said, running over to me and grabbing me around the waist.

"He's not?" I asked, peeling Gabbi off me and pulling up a stool. "Where is he?"

"We thought he was with you," Mrs. Ormond replied. She put her dish towel down and peered at me, forcing a tiny crease across her brow. "He said you were all coming over for a midnight movie last night."

"Yeah," I nodded. "Right."

"And I figured all of you—"

We were interrupted by the front door creaking open.

"Cal?" Mrs. Ormond called out, her face growing increasingly concerned.

Ever since Cal had been back home, and Mrs. Ormond had been weaned off the toxins Rafe had been secretly feeding her, she'd been keeping pretty close tabs on Cal's whereabouts. Cal could barely pee without her knowing about it.

"It's just me," said Winter, slowly walking in and easing her bag off her shoulder. "Sorry," she added, sensing everyone's disappointment. She shrugged as she looked at me and then at the others. "I came here looking for Cal, too."

Mrs. Ormond quickly walked off towards the theater room and returned with Cal's phone in her hand. "I thought I heard it ringing earlier today," she said, looking at it in confusion. "I don't know how to work this thing!"

Gabbi slid off her stool and grabbed the phone from her mum. "Where is he?" Gabbi asked, staring at me and Winter, willing us to give her an answer. "There are missed calls here from both of you. Where has he gone? He never leaves his phone behind. Mum?" she asked, looking for reassurance.

"I don't know," Mrs. Ormond replied. Her face wrinkled more deeply with worry. "This isn't like Cal. I assumed he was with one of you." She paused to look at Winter and then at me. "But I shouldn't have assumed anything," she continued, berating herself. Her hands were trembling. Out of the corner of my eye, I noticed Winter nervously watching them, too.

Mrs. Ormond reached for a glass of water by the sink, but her quivering fingers knocked it straight to the floor. The glass shattered loudly, sending jagged pieces shooting across the tiles.

She watched the explosion at her feet. Once the last shard had settled, she looked at us with red, watery eyes.

"It's OK," said Winter, grabbing the broom and dustpan from beside the fridge. "I've got it. Gab, watch your bare feet. Boges?"

I took my cue from Winter and gave Gabbi a piggyback, carrying her out of the kitchen and plonking her down on the living room couch.

"Cal's probably just at Ryan's," I called out. "Nothing to worry about."

"Actually, I think he did say something about watching movies at Ryan's," said Winter.

"Oh? But I thought you—" I started to say, until I noticed Winter's desperate eye signals. "Oh, yeah, that's right," I added, hoping my recovery didn't sound too lame. "He did say something about that."

I hoped our lies would settle the uneasy feeling that was hanging in the air at the Ormond household.

For now, at least.

Gab got up from the couch and turned off the nearby TV. "But why would he go to Ryan's when he can watch movies here?" She pulled her hair back into a ponytail and gestured towards the new theater room.

"Maybe to get away from a pesky little sister?" I teased playfully.

Winter carefully tipped the glassy contents of the dustpan into a trash bag. "How about I just duck out, ring Ryan and ask him?" she said, grabbing her shoulder bag and wandering towards the sliding door to the backyard. She didn't wait for any of us to answer.

"Come on, Gab, help me with this garlic bread, please," said Mrs. Ormond. Gab stepped into her slippers, and the pair turned their attention back to dinner.

I flicked the TV on again, then walked to the sliding door that looked over the backyard. I made a gap in the vertical drapes and scanned the shadowy view. The moon was high in the sky. Winter was in the far corner of the backyard, on the phone, head down, kicking at the barbecue with her boot.

She must have sensed me watching and turned around.

I opened my eyes wide, as if to ask, *So, does Ryan know anything?*

She looked back with dark, worried eyes, then scrunched up her face and shook her head.

Where *was* Cal?

I backed away from the door and glanced around the living room. The cluster of picture frames on the wall had grown a lot this year. The commando angel Cal's dad had drawn hung in a dark wood frame, next to a new photo of Ryan. There was also a cool shot of Repro in his underground river canoe, standing up with a long oar, like a gondolier.

My line of sight stopped on a photo of Tom, Cal's dad. For the last few months I'd hardly been able to look at it. A couple of times I'd glanced at it really quickly, and fear had almost floored me as visions of Rafe, Tom's identical twin and the mastermind behind his death, flashed into my mind. Again, I could see him staring up at us from beneath the massive Ormond Angel statue that had fallen on him at the Cragkill Keep ruins. Rafe was a murderer, willing to wipe out his own brother and nephew because of his rage and envy at not being the heir to the Ormond inheritance. Rafe had nearly killed us all—Cal, me *and* Winter—in Ireland. That intense, evil glint in his eye was impossible to forget.

I closed my own eyes for a second and forced myself to think of happier things.

I looked at the picture again. Tom's eyes were different. There was a fire in them, but his was a fire that said he'd do anything for his family.

Cal had completed Tom's mission for him, uncovered the DMO (Dangerous Mystery of the Ormonds) and had reunited the family by finding his brother, Ryan, and bringing his mum and Gabbi back together again in the family home. It must have been so strange for Ryan and Cal—getting used to being identical twins. But Ryan seemed pretty cool about it all. He was fitting into the family almost like he'd always been around.

Now we just had to figure out where Cal had gone.

I tried to shake off my nerves and headed

back into the kitchen. Mrs. Ormond and Gab were cutting up garlic bread. "Need any help?" I asked, and both jumped slightly at the sound of my voice. "A taste-tester, maybe?"

"Sorry, Boges, did you say something?" Mrs. Ormond said.

At that moment, the sliding door opened, and Winter walked in with a broad smile on her face. She rubbed her silver love-heart locket between her fingers. "All good," she announced. "He's over at Ryan's. He left his phone here last night by accident. Boges," she said, turning to me with an awkward, I-hate-lying look in her eyes, "want to go over and join them?"

"Sounds good to me. I'm sure Gab and Mrs. O. can arrange my dinner to go . . ."

Mrs. Ormond smiled, shaking her head at me playfully as she pulled on red polka-dot oven mitts and lifted the steaming lasagna pan out of the oven. "Tell Cal to call me when you see him, will you? Make sure you take his phone, too."

"Cool, will do, Mrs. Ormond," said Winter. "Boges, you sort yourself and your stomach out, I'm just going to run up to Cal's room—I think I left my pink sweater up there the other day. Back in a sec."

Since Winter had been going out with Cal,

she'd definitely been looking more girly. She was even wearing a dress the other day, with all these lacy ruffles around the neck. But, in true Winter style, she'd teamed it with her black boots. I couldn't recall her ever wearing a pink sweater, though.

Gab cut me a huge slab of lasagna and lifted it into a container. Cheesy threads stretched across the kitchen counter. "Might as well take some extra for Cal and Ryan," she said.

"You will share with them, won't you, Boges?" added Mrs. Ormond with a wink. "And can you let Janet know we'd love to see her and Ryan on the weekend sometime, if they're free?"

"Sure thing, Mrs. O.," I said. I hoped this was the last lie I would tell to her, and that Cal would show up soon, but something was telling me it wouldn't be that simple.

"Got it," said Winter, jumping down the last couple of stairs. "See you two again soon?" she said, giving Cal's mum and sister kisses on the cheek.

"Yep," said Gab. "You promised we'd have another Pictionary night soon, right?"

"You're on. C'mon, Boges." Winter grabbed my arm and headed for the door. I followed her, swiftly scooping up the lasagna and Cal's phone on my way out.

Winter was practically running down the driveway.

"Wait up!" I called, jogging to catch up. "What did Ryan really say?"

"He has no idea where Cal is," she said, stopping to face me. "No idea! He hasn't heard anything since yesterday. Just like us."

I could feel my palms getting clammy and quickly wiped them on the back of my jeans. "Well, he's probably just—"

"Just what?" Winter snapped. "Just what, Boges? Taken time out? Time out from what? Yeah, the paparazzi have been a nightmare, but he spent a year on the run, and all he wanted was to be back with his family. Cal would *not* want time out from this," she said, circling in the cool, crisp air of Flood Street.

"But—"

"But, nothing." Even though it was dark outside, I could see that Winter's eyes were bloodshot. "I'm sorry," she said, shaking her head. "It's just . . . it's not good, Boges. Something's wrong. I'm sure of it."

"It hasn't even been one day. He could be at Repro's. He'll show up." Even though I felt the same, something about Winter always made me want to argue with her.

She held a clenched fist in front of her.

"I know what you're thinking," she said. "You always think I'm paranoid, just like Cal does. But this is different. Since we've been back, there hasn't been a day when Cal and I haven't at least checked in with each other."

She opened her palm, and I squinted to see what she was holding. It looked like a small disc.

"I found this in Cal's room . . ." she began, before we were interrupted by the sound of crunching leaves nearby. "What was that?"

We both spun around to try to locate the source of the sound.

Silence took over again.

"Probably just a possum," I suggested.

I picked up the disc from her open palm. It was a red wax seal that looked like it had come off the back of an envelope. Stamped into the wax was a picture of a falling angel. It looked like the Ormond Angel, from Cragkill Keep, only this one looked frightened and defeated, its huge wings clearly battered and broken. I turned it over. A torn film of creamy paper clung to the back.

I looked up at Winter, confused. "I don't get it. What is this?"

"I don't know, but I'd like to find out. I just found it in Cal's room, on the floor by the window. I went upstairs to see if his bag was still there."

"And?"

"His bag was under his desk, where he always leaves it."

"So he's taken off without his bag, without his phone . . . what about his wallet?"

Winter shook her head. "He must have it with him. At least, I *hope* he has it with him."

I held the wax seal up to the light for a closer look.

"Weird, right?" Winter asked. "Cal disappears without a word, leaves his phone and his bag, and then I find that on the floor. What do you think it's from? What does it mean?"

I didn't know the answer to that. And I didn't like it. The image of the angel was too close to home. Especially when no one knew where Cal was.

I handed the seal back to Winter. Once more, I felt a lie slip from my lips. "Don't read into it. It's probably nothing."

I could tell by the way her dark eyes were glazing over that she didn't believe it was nothing. "You don't think it has anything to do with that Willoughby guy, do you? Pulling another stupid stunt?"

"No, I'm pretty sure he learned his lesson after last time. There's no way Cal would let him off the hook again, and he knows that. His career would be over."

There was this local journalist, Ben Willoughby, who'd been hanging around Cal's place like a bad smell. First, we caught him spray-painting "No Psycho" on the Ormonds' garage. Next, he tried to talk to Gabbi just outside the house, asking her about that day last year when she was attacked—the day Cal's life on the run began. Luckily, Ryan saw Gab being hassled so he tackled Ben and grabbed him in a headlock, refusing to let go until he explained what he was doing. It turned out the Ormond story had "gone quiet," and Willoughby was trying to liven it up with something he thought would get Cal angry, giving him something to write about.

We wanted to take it to the police, but Cal refused, telling Ryan to let it go. He didn't want to give the media what they wanted—another story.

Winter put her hands on her hips and sighed. "So what do we do, Boges?"

"I think we just have to wait. You saw the look on Mrs. O.'s face tonight when she thought Cal had run off. As soon as she sensed something was up, she started crumbling. It's been so long since she was . . . like that. She's just getting her life back on track, and I don't think it would take much to send her spiraling again. We have to convince her everything's fine until Cal shows up. OK?"

"Just call me if he turns up at the lab tomorrow . . . please?"

"I'm sure he will," I said unconvincingly.

Home
Dorothy Road, Richmond

9:53 pm

I switched on Cal's phone, and a photo of his mum, sister and girlfriend stared back at me. Quickly, I typed out a message.

My stomach churned as my finger hovered over "send," and that wasn't because of all the piroshki I ate after devouring Mrs. Ormond's lasagna earlier. I hated not knowing where Cal was, and my interview nerves were getting worse. Even though Cal had offered me anything I wanted from the Ormond fortune, I wanted to land the NASA internship and make it on my own terms.

I really didn't like what I was about to do, but I was doing it for my best friend.

I finally pressed "send."

📱 hi mum, going to crash at ryan's tonight. we're watching movies. c u tomorrow.

Just a minute later, Cal's phone beeped, alerting me to an incoming message.

📱 ok honey. say hi to your brother for me. have fun and don't stay up too late. you have to go to school tomorrow for that group assignment, remember. we missed you today. love you lots, mum and gab xx

It had only been a day, I told myself. Cal was big enough to take one day out without having to tell us about it.

I'd see him in the morning at school—a few of us were meeting up to get a head start on a group science project due next term. Cal would tell me he'd just needed a break, or that he'd lost track of time helping out Repro with some sort of crazy project in his new place . . . or that he'd gone to visit that Melba Snipe lady who had helped him when he was on the run. I glared at my textbooks, still sitting in that stack. I'd lied to Mum and Gran tonight about studying. I'd done nothing since I got home from Cal's but check my emails, stare at my fish tank and watch my phone, willing it to ring.

But no matter how hard I tried to convince

myself, and Winter, that Cal was OK—wherever he was—I couldn't shake the sick feeling in my stomach.

I tossed and turned in bed just as I had those nights, months ago, when I hadn't heard from Cal for days and had no idea where he was . . . or whether he was even still alive.

I broke out in a sweat, a familiar feeling resurfacing.

Fear.

DAY 2

29 days to go . . .

Cal's House
Flood Street, Richmond

7:30 pm

I huddled behind the bushes, waiting outside for Winter. I didn't want to walk in on my own and have to deal with Gab and Mrs. O.'s questions.

All day long my eyes had darted back and forth towards the lab door. But Cal never showed. I told everyone he was sick, and that he'd promised to make up for his part of the assignment another day. I guess it was obvious my mind was elsewhere because everyone kept asking me if I was OK.

Winter had phoned about a dozen times, and she'd convinced me to meet her again at Flood Street. As much as neither of us wanted to admit to Mrs. O. that we had no idea where her son was, we had to tell her. She was going to flip out, but we just didn't know what else to do.

Leaves rustled again, like we'd heard last night. I glanced around, looking for Winter. In the bushes on the other side of the driveway, I spotted movement.

"Hey," I said firmly, walking over. "Who's there?"

The figure slowly retreated.

"Cal?" I asked. "Is that—" A car drove by on the street behind me, its headlights momentarily lighting up the dark figure. "Willoughby!" I shouted, lunging at him. The journalist groaned and kicked out in shock as I grabbed him in a headlock, like I'd seen Ryan do. "What do you think you're doing here?!"

"Get off me!"

"I thought we told you already to get the—" The Ormonds' entrance light suddenly came on. I covered Willoughby's mouth and pulled him down, out of sight. "Shh!" I hissed, as he struggled and groaned.

I gasped as he bit hard on my fingers in reply.

Gabbi's face appeared at the front door. She stepped out and looked around the front yard. Her hair was loose, hanging around her shoulders. She was wearing an oversized pair of blue-and-white striped pajamas and Ugg boots.

Then, satisfied that nothing unusual was

going on, she went back inside and closed the door while I struggled to contain Willoughby.

I loosened my grip around his mouth. "What do you think you're doing out here?"

He shoved me away, and I fell into a thorny rose bush. He was small and scrawny-looking, but seriously strong. I jumped back onto my feet and towered over him.

"Answer me," I said. I grabbed the collar of his shirt with both hands. "What are you doing here, hiding in the bushes?"

"I just—"

At that moment, Winter ran up the driveway, right over to us, and wrenched Ben Willoughby clean out of my grip. "What is *this*," she said, pulling the journalist away, "doing on Cal's property again?"

A black camera crashed to the ground, and Winter kicked it hard across the road and under a streetlight. It collided with the curb, and the lens cracked loudly. The shutter clicked senselessly.

Willoughby yelled and shook himself free. "You can pay for that!" he said, scowling at his damaged camera. He straightened his light gray shirt that was now smeared with grass stains and combed back his black hair with his hands as I sized him up. He was probably only a few years older than me. His weaselly lime-green eyes glared out of black-rimmed glasses that appeared to be more for looking cool than for improving his vision.

"What do you want with Cal?" I snapped. "Can't you just leave him and his family alone? Don't you think he's been through enough?"

"I'm just trying to do my job," he said through gritted teeth. "The *Psycho Kid*'s not here, anyway," he added. "I haven't seen him since the other night."

Winter stepped up to him again. "What do you mean, 'the other night'?"

Willoughby smirked, clearly enjoying antagonizing us. "I *mean*, I haven't seen him since the other night. It was around midnight, and he came out here yelling about me leaving him some sort of note."

"*Note*?" I asked. "You'd better keep talking, dude, or we'll call the police."

Willoughby smirked again. "Go ahead. I'm sure they'll be interested in how my camera ended up smashed on the roadside."

"Yeah, and I'm sure they'll want to know about you harassing Gabbi—a kid—just for a lead, won't they?" I retorted. I pulled out my phone and started dialing.

"OK, OK," he quickly agreed. "Chill out."

"So, talk!"

"I'd been up at the local gas station, covering a story on last week's armed holdup—"

"Sounds riveting," I said.

He scowled at me again before continuing. "And when I was done there, I decided to swing by Flood Street on my way home. As I was *strolling* by, Cal came charging out of the house, shouting and carrying on."

"Why was he shouting? What did you do to him?"

"I hadn't done anything. Some car had slowed down out in front of his house, so of course he instantly thinks it's the paparazzi, out to get him. Then he starts shouting *my* name, accusing *me* of sending him a note."

Winter backed away, looking down at the ground, as we both tried desperately to process what Willoughby was saying.

Someone had sent Cal a note. A threatening note. A note sealed with an impression of a falling angel?

"And then what?" I said.

"And then nothing. I took off." Willoughby's voice suddenly dropped in tone. "Why, what's happened to him? Where is he?" He dug into his pocket and pulled out a tiny recording device, swiftly activating it with his thumb. He waved it in our faces. "Do you know where he is, Bodhan? Winter?"

Winter swung at him, but he jerked the recorder out of her reach.

"So where's Cal?" he taunted. "Clearly you're both worried. I thought he'd want to be with his family, after tearing their lives apart."

"You'd better shut your mouth right now," Winter threatened.

"Well, he did fly all the way to Ireland to kill his uncle . . . not to mention your former guardian, Vulkan Sligo, who you all watched suffocate to death in the mud."

"Winter, don't listen to him," I said.

"And *Sumo*," said Willoughby, "who also suffered a muddy demise, as I recall. And let's not forget the Zombrovski brothers! One plunged from a bell tower and broke his neck, thanks to Ormond, the other joined Sumo and Sligo in the mud. Sheldrake Rathbone—bog. Nelson Sharkey—crushed by earthmover—"

"Enough!" Winter's face was furious. She swung at him again . . . and missed.

"He's just trying to get a reaction out of us," I said, to calm her down. "Everyone knows the true story now. Don't listen to him."

"So where is he?" Willoughby asked again, swinging the recorder over to me. "Who's next on Cal's hit list? Maybe Ryan, or should I say,

Sam? I bet Cal doesn't like sharing his mother's affections, hmm? And Boges? Could *you* be next? You seem to be spending a lot of late nights with Winter recently . . ."

I swatted the recorder away and grabbed at his collar again. "He's taken off to get a break from people like you," I said. "Now, you better get out of here before I really call the cops."

8:03 pm

Ben Willoughby's rant had left us reeling. I didn't care what he had to say about the people who'd been killed during the search for the DMO. I was only interested in the note.

Cal was normally so careful whenever he thought a photographer or a reporter was nearby. What kind of note could have tempted him out of the house at midnight, hurling abuse into the darkness? Why was the note stamped with an image of a falling angel? And if Willoughby wasn't behind it, then who was?

"We can't go inside now and face Mrs. O. with all this," I said.

Winter nodded. "We need to figure out what's going on first. Why don't I check in with Ryan again, and maybe Griff Kirby, too?" said Winter. "See if they've heard anything."

"OK, I'll head over to Repro's, just in case Cal's there. And when I get home, I'll run some online checks to see whether he's used his ATM card somewhere."

Winter smiled hopefully. "So what will we do about Mrs. Ormond tonight?" she asked, before we separated. "We can't just ignore her. She'll freak out if she doesn't hear from Cal again."

"I'll look after it," I whispered. I wrapped my arms around my friend and patted her back. She was shivering. "And don't worry about Cal. Maybe he'd reached breaking point with everyone being so in his face about his story, especially if Willoughby spouted any of that insane garbage to him. You know what it's been like for us—I can't tell you the amount of times my *gran* has been stopped at the grocery store and asked whether she's the grandmother of the 'Psycho Kid's' best friend. It's crazy! And Cal has been copping it way worse—he must just need some time out."

Winter pulled away from me. "Boges, I'm not an idiot. And I know you're not, either. You don't even believe what you're saying right now! You're scratching your head and doing that nervous cough. There's no way Cal would put us through this again. No way. We both know that. Something seriously bad is going on. I knew this was coming."

"What do you mean?"

"You know I haven't felt right since leaving Ireland. The whole 365-day nightmare doesn't feel over. Sure, I have my house back, plus the other Frey properties . . . but my mum and dad are gone forever. Cal started feeling like his old self again as soon as he was back home in Richmond, but for me it's different. Maybe it's because I couldn't go back to having my family like he could."

Winter pulled her jacket up around her chin and shuddered.

"I don't know if it's because Vulkan taught me to be distrustful, wary and, well, paranoid," she said, "but . . . I still watch my back, Boges."

8:22 pm

As I walked away from Flood Street, I held Cal's phone in my hand, steeling myself to lie to his mum once more.

📱 hi mum, just me again. so sorry I haven't been home. was caught up at the library with boges. i'm at his house now, helping him with a new project. ok if i stay here tonight? I think it will be a late one . . .

Again a reply came back with supersonic speed, making me feel worse.

📱 ok love . . . but please come home for dinner tomorrow night. gab is dying to see you. we both are. maybe we could ask ryan over too. i'll call him in the morning. mum xx

Repro's House
Florence Street, Central

9:17 pm

Cal had given Repro enough money to set himself up in a tall, narrow row house near City Hall. The place had a front door, just like anywhere else, but Repro was still trying to get used to the idea of using it. We'd helped him paint the place and tidy it up. We'd even built a loft on the top floor, which he'd started to fill with what remained of his collection. The rest of the place was clean and tidy and spacious—far from what Repro was used to!

I made a face under the front sensor light when I felt Repro peering at me through the peephole.

"The filing cabinet entrance sounded cooler," I said, when he opened the door.

"I think so, too," said Repro, with a laugh. He moved aside and let me through.

I took a few steps and stopped, staring around in disbelief.

Repro came up beside me and rocked back

and forth proudly. "Once a collector, always a collector!" he proclaimed.

I didn't recognize the place. We could have been in a hide-out in the complex underground rail network, or in a dank lair only accessible by canoe. Repro's mountains of stuff had returned.

"But where's the furniture we bought? The couch, the coffee table? The bookshelves? I can't see anything but . . . stuff!" There were books on astronomy, boxes of old film reels, shipping magazines, wooden owl statues. And jars of . . . jars of—"Repro, what *are* these things?"

"Eyeballs," Repro replied. "Well, glass eyes. Everything else is still here, don't worry," he said, tugging back a plaid picnic blanket like a magician. "See?"

Papers fluttered to the floor, and reels of thread in a rainbow of colors rolled away as he revealed part of the new couch.

"Cuppa?" he asked, tiptoeing over the junk to where the kitchen once was.

"Um, no thanks," I said. I picked up a handful of mail that was scattered on the floor at my feet and flicked through the envelopes aimlessly.

"So, what seems to be the trouble? Or is this just a social visit?" Repro asked, as he gestured towards an old-fashioned printing press, wanting me to help him move it.

"It's Cal," I replied. "He's not buried in here somewhere, is he?"

"Afraid not. Why? What's happened?"

I explained the missing Cal situation as we inched the press over to its new resting spot near a window, kicking stuff out of the way in the process.

Repro listened intently. He brushed the dust from his hands as he stood there nodding solemnly in his fluffy yellow bathrobe.

"Well, if I hear anything I'll send one of my pigeons out with the message," he said.

I eyed him suspiciously. Nothing would surprise me with this guy.

"Just messing with you. I don't have a pigeon coop . . . yet," Repro said. "But I will let you know if I hear from young Cal. You'll let me know too, when he shows up? I hope he hasn't met with foul play," he added.

"So, have you tracked down your mum yet?" I asked, changing the subject. Cal had told me just the other day that Repro was afraid his mum wouldn't want to know him after all the years that had passed and all his run-ins with the law.

Repro shook his head. "No, no, no. Hasn't been time for that."

"Maybe soon," I said, getting ready to leave.

"By the way," I added, "who's Albert? I saw the name on those letters over there. Is he the guy who lived here before you moved in?"

"Ah, no," he replied bashfully. "Er, Albert is me."

DAY 3

28 days to go . . .

Home
Dorothy Road, Richmond

7:15 am

"Bodhan, wake up. Bodhan!"

"What? What is it, Mama?" I asked, pulling my blanket over my head to block out the light. "I'm sleeping!"

"Winifred Ormond is here to see you," she said, shaking my shoulder firmly.

"What?"

"Quick, Bodhan, get up!"

I launched myself out of bed and pulled on the gray sweatpants that were slung over my desk chair. I got one leg stuck and hopping off-balance, crushed some audio equipment on the floor and almost slammed into my fish tank.

"Please," I heard Mrs. Ormond's muffled pleading from down the hall. "I need to know where my son is! I need to speak to Boges, now! Boges! I want the truth!"

"Tell her I'm not here!" I hissed to my mum.

"What do you mean, Bodhan? What's going on?"

"Please, Mama, I'll explain later. I have to go. I'm really, really sorry." My mum stared at me, shocked and confused, as I threw some stuff in my bag, kicked the screen out of my bedroom window frame, then jumped out into the back-yard.

I fell hard on the dewy grass—it had been a while since I'd had to sneak out my window. I crawled to my feet and looked up at Mum again. She was staring down, her eyes wide. I held my hands up to calm her, then held a finger to my lips. "I'll be back soon," I mouthed, "I promise!"

7:34 am

When I finally stopped running and slowed down to grab a breather, I regretted my decision to bolt out of the house. I wasn't ready to face Mrs. Ormond, but now I'd upset my mum, too. I'd seriously betrayed her trust last year when I snuck out of the country to Ireland, and I promised I'd never lie to her *ever* again . . .

And then I spotted the newspaper headlines.

FORMER TEEN FUGITIVE CAL ORMOND ON THE RUN AGAIN

Best friend, Bodhan "Boges" Michalko, claims Ormond is fed up with life in the limelight and as a result has "taken off."

I didn't need to see any more than that. Ben Willoughby! Why couldn't he leave Cal alone? My mind reeled. No wonder Mrs. Ormond had come after me, wanting answers.

I wanted answers, too. I'd tried everything I could think of. But I hadn't found a trace of Cal anywhere.

Where could he be?

Winter's House
Mansfield Way, Dolphin Point

2:13 pm

Winter and I sat on her couches, staring off into

space. Neither of us knew what to do about Cal, and we felt absolutely useless. I was meant to be preparing for my NASA interview, but I couldn't concentrate on that when the only problem I wanted to solve was finding out what had happened to my best friend.

We were clutching to the idea that Cal had taken time out, but neither of us really believed it. I looked over at Winter, still in her pajamas. She was practically strangling a cushion, her brow furrowed.

She'd moved back into the Frey house months ago, but so far only had the basics organized. The place was well over ten times the size of her old rooftop apartment in Lesley Street, and I don't know if it was the emptiness, but Winter looked small and pale. I offered her some of my ham and cheese sandwich, but she refused it with the tiniest shake of her head.

We both jumped when her cell phone rang from the coffee table.

"Who is it?" I said, as she looked at the screen.

"Don't know. No caller ID."

Tentatively, she pressed the "answer" button. "Hello?"

Winter's face instantly transformed from worried to horrified. Her shoulders tensed up around her ears, and her mouth fell open.

"What's wrong? Who is it?" I asked, rushing to her side.

"Who is this?" she said, her voice trembling.

"Put it on speakerphone," I whispered.

With shaking hands, Winter held her phone out and activated the speaker.

"You do not need to know that right now," answered a distorted, robotic voice. "All you need to know is that I have Cal."

Hearing the caller speak Cal's name was like being punched in the gut. I leaned on the coffee table, forcing myself to focus and listen to what they had to say.

"Look in your mailbox," the distorted voice ordered. "Take what you find and give it to his mother. Tell her he gave it to you—it should keep her quiet for a while. Do as I say, and I will show your friend to you."

"Why? What's in there?" Winter cried. "Is Cal OK?"

"Breathe a word of this to the authorities, and something very bad will happen to your friend," the sinister voice continued.

"Where is Cal? What have you done to him?"

"Once you've made the delivery, go straight to the clock tower. There, you'll be given further instructions. Do it now!"

The call ended.

I was stunned by the words. Frozen. Winter grabbed her coat, her bag and her boots and ran for the door. "Come on!" she shouted, glaring back at me.

Cal's House
Flood Street, Richmond

3:35 pm

Dear Mum and Gab,

Sorry I took off without talking to you first. Life has been tough lately. I'm not coping. Gotta take a break for a while. Only a few days or so to get some space from all the attention.

Love Cal

Mrs. Ormond burst into tears as she read Cal's letter—the letter that we knew had been delivered to Winter's house by some unknown abductor.

"But he seemed so happy," she cried. "Everything was going so well. The attention has been tough, I know, but I thought he was coping."

Winter handed Mrs. Ormond a box of tissues. Mrs. O. had come so far since her dark days with Rafe and his mind-altering potions, but right now she looked almost as frail as she had last year. I held Gabbi tightly as she, too, cried into a tissue.

"I've been trying so hard to make it up to him," continued Mrs. Ormond. She dropped her head into her hands. "But how could he ever forgive me for not believing him last year?"

"This has nothing to do with you," Winter offered, "*or* Gab. I promise. It's just . . ." Winter stopped and wrapped her arms around Mrs. Ormond's slumped shoulders. "It's just that the press still follow him everywhere he goes . . . and he just needs some time out. He'll be back before we know it, I promise."

Gab pulled away from me, leaving behind a big, damp spot on my T-shirt. "But where is he?" she asked. "Who's looking after him?"

I could barely speak. I looked at Winter. The

threat made by the kidnapper was all I could think of. Cal was in mortal danger, forced to write a fake note. I scratched my head and sighed.

Solving complex equations and tampering with technology to get me out of the trickiest of situations was easy, but when it came to making up stories about the whereabouts of my best friend . . . my mind was drawing a blank.

Luckily, Winter was a better liar. "You both remember hearing about Melba Snipe, right?" she said, trying to make her voice sound calm. "That sweet old lady who helped Cal when he was on the run? Well, he's camped up at her place for a while. No big deal. But you can't tell this to anyone, OK? He's trying to get *out* of the spotlight."

"But can't we go and see him?" cried Gabbi. "At night, even?"

I frowned and shook my head.

"I can't believe this is happening again," Gab added.

"It's not *happening again*," I said. "This is different. We just need to give him some space."

Winter fiddled with her earrings—two pairs of silver swallows, joined in flight. The four of us looked to the floor, despairing for different reasons. But one thing remained the same. Cal was gone.

5:09 pm

People pointed and muttered as Winter and I passed them on the street. Usually I didn't mind the attention so much—these days everyone at school treated me like a rock star, and as if I'd complain about that.

But today was different. We had no idea who had taken Cal, or why.

"Boges!" a voice called out. I gulped as I turned and found Madeleine Baker running up to me.

Winter stopped a few feet ahead of me and watched impatiently, hands on her hips.

Maddy and I had been hanging out with each other a lot lately, but I'd barely had time to think about her the last few days.

"Hey, stranger," she said, tugging on the thin white cords of her headphones, popping them out of her ears and leaving them hanging over her top. She smiled uncertainly, her freckled cheeks pink from running. "Boges, are you OK?"

"Um, sure," I said, straightening up. "I just . . ."

"You were supposed to meet me earlier today. For a run," she added, looking down at her running shorts and shoes.

"Oh," I said slowly. "Sorry. I just—"

I knew I had to keep my mouth shut. I couldn't tell her anything.

Maddy looked ahead at Winter, then back at me.

Winter was glaring at me in the distance. She jabbed at her watch. She'd been the one who'd pushed me to ask out Maddy in the first place, but right now it was clear she didn't care about anything or anyone but Cal. And neither did I.

I stepped back.

"What is it?" Maddy persisted.

"I'm sorry . . ." I took a deep breath to brace myself. "I can't deal with this right now."

She stared at me, confused. "What do you mean? You want to break up?" she asked.

Before I had a chance to answer, she turned and jogged away from me.

Clock Tower

5:39 pm

We sat on the ground, silent. No one was around— it was eerily quiet. We just had to wait for the caller to contact us again.

Winter must have snuck Cal's letter back into her pocket after showing it to his mum and Gab. She was clutching it, reading it over and over again.

"What are you looking for?" I asked. "A secret message to decipher with the Caesar shift?" I joked nervously. "I don't think Cal could have been in a position to pull that off."

143

"You never know," she said.

"What do you mean?"

Winter ignored me. I could see her mouthing Cal's words as if they would somehow tell her where he was.

"Oriana's in jail," I said, my mind desperately trying to work out who was behind Cal's kidnapping. "Sligo, Sumo, Zombie One and Zombie Two are all dead. What about Red Tank Top?" But I knew that was unlikely.

I felt hopeless just waiting for something to happen.

"We're here!" I said out loud, to our unknown enemy. "We did what we were told! Where are you? Show yourself!"

A sudden puff of air shot past my ear, and I looked up. Winter stared at me, shocked, then her eyes closed, and she slumped to the side.

As I lurched forward to catch her, there was another rush of air, and I felt a shooting pain in my arm. I looked at Winter, confused. Before I knew it, I was slumping over to join her.

UnKnown Location

8:54 pm

Dazed, I opened my eyes, trying to get my bearings. Something was jabbing me in my side.

"Boges, wake up. Boges?"

"What happened?" I moaned, squirming away from Winter's prodding. Slowly everything was coming into focus, like a thick fog lifting.

Winter's face came into view. Her eyes were red and panicked. My head was heavy as I turned and took in our surroundings.

"Where are we?"

"I don't know, but we have to get out. Come on," she prompted, grabbing my hands and trying to help me to my feet. "Are you OK?"

"Yeah, you?"

"I'll be better when I find out what's going on."

I managed to sit up, but everything was shaking. We were in some sort of dark, damp room, with a dirt floor. I could have kicked myself. *Go to the clock tower,* he'd said. And we'd done just that. Walked straight into a trap.

I peered around, shining my key light over the room. With the small circle of light, I traced the join of two dank concrete walls. In another corner there was a wire snaking up to a speaker at the ceiling. A humming sound buzzed into my ears. What the? . . .

Suddenly a bluish light came on behind me. Winter grabbed my hand, and we spun around. High on the wall was a TV screen. We approached it, squinting, trying to make sense of the blurry shape—a figure huddled in the dark corner of what looked like a shed.

"Boges, what's going on?" Winter cried, squeezing my arm.

"I don't know, but this is freaking me out."

The figure on the screen looked up.

"No!" Winter shrieked, falling to her knees and grabbing at the screen. "No, no, no! It's Cal! Where is he?!"

"Cal!" I shouted. What I was seeing couldn't be real!

"What have they done to him?" Winter pleaded.

"Winter?" Cal whispered, barely moving. His weak voice spluttered through the speaker in the corner of the room. "Winter?"

"He can hear us! Cal! It's me and Boges!" she answered. "Are you OK?"

"Cal, it's Boges," I said, as calmly as I could. "You need to tell us where you are."

"I—I don't know . . . where I am," said Cal softly, slowly turning his head. His eyes strained to focus on his surroundings. Dirty blond hair streaked down his face, damp and stringy. "I . . . can't . . . I don't know," he repeated.

"That's OK, buddy," I said. "We'll find you, and we'll get you out. Don't worry."

"You're *here*?" said Cal, suddenly lurching forward on his hands and knees, looking around himself frantically. The sound of metal scraping the ground grated into our ears. His leg was shackled. "I knew you'd find me . . . I knew you'd work it out. I can hear—" Cal fell back again, coughing.

The horrible hacking sound spat out of the speaker and reverberated around the room.

"We'll get you out of there, OK?" I said, barely able to breathe, let alone speak. I was vaguely aware of Winter muttering something, over and over, beside me. "Just tell us what you can," I said, "and we'll find you."

"*Work it out?*" Winter cried. "Work it out? What do you mean, Cal? Work out where you are? Who has you? What do you mean?"

The picture shook and shifted, snatching Cal from us as though someone had batted the camera lens away from him. Then the live video feed cut out with a piercing noise, and the room was plunged into darkness once more.

"Work it out?" Winter muttered again. I could hear her scrambling for something in her pocket. "His letter, Boges. Quick, give me some light!"

I shone my key light on her as she searched through Cal's crumpled words once more.

The paper shook as her hands trembled. She'd found something in there. Something bad.

"Tell me!" I said. "What is it?"

Her face was grim with fear. "I knew it," she whispered. "I *knew* he'd try to get a message to us, no matter how dangerous. It's the letters at the start of each sentence."

Winter's voice trembled as she slowly and quietly read out five deadly words: "Sorry . . . Life . . . I'm . . . Gotta . . . Only . . . S—L—I—G—O!" she shouted. "Sligo's alive! *Sligo* has him!"

"That's right!" the familiar voice roared, throbbing through the speaker above us. "Back from the dead!"

We swung around.

Scowling back at us, in close-up on the screen, was the round, repulsive, fleshy face of Vulkan Sligo!

One eye bulged like a toad's, while the other was half-closed and perched uselessly above a deep purple scar on his cheek. He wore his characteristic cravat around his neck, yet this one was stained and dull, nothing like the perfect silks I'd seen choking him before.

This was Sligo, all right, but a Sligo who looked like he'd been dragged through . . . *the mud.*

I cowered away from his terrifying image, pulling Winter close to me.

"I knew you were still alive!" she gasped. "You're like a cockroach that just won't die! Where have you taken Cal?"

"What kind of a 'welcome back' reception do you call that?" he spat. "Hardly what I'd expect from the poor little orphan I raised in my own home."

"Your home? It was *my* home! You murdered my parents, and you stole everything from us!"

His mouth tightened back into a scowl.

"Listen very carefully," Sligo instructed. "Cal has been injected with a lethal dose of poison."

"You poisoned him?" Winter cried. "With what?"

My entire skull was pounding as the camera angle changed, and Cal's slumped head came back into view, his body motionless.

"Cal!" I shouted, trying to get a reaction. "Cal!"

He seemed to move—his fingers twitched—but before I could tell for sure, the camera returned to Sligo.

"Your friend's days are numbered," he said. "If you continue to do what I say, I will give him the antidote. If you run to the authorities, or do anything not strictly according to my wishes, I will inject him with a second dose of poison that will have fatal results . . . within seconds."

"We won't tell a soul—we just want Cal back!" I shouted. "But what do you want from us? Money? Whatever it is, we'll get it to you. Just don't let anything happen to Cal," I pleaded. "We'll get you anything you want!"

Sligo gritted his yellow, rotting teeth. Spittle flew from his sausage-like lips. "You three *stole* the Ormond Jewel from me and snatched the Ormond Singularity from my grasp. You destroyed my dreams of ruling the city and gaining the respect and admiration I deserved. You ruined my name and my empire. But you won't ruin me. I will make a return. I will find a way. But first, I need money. And lots of it."

"Fine," I said, squeezing Winter's hand and willing her to keep her mouth shut. "We'll get you as much as you want."

"Yes, you will," he nodded. "I will send for you again when your instructions are ready."

Winter shook my hand away. "Ready? When will they be ready? Just tell us what you want now!"

The screen went blank.

Only the rasping voice remained, hanging in the darkness as Sligo hissed, "If you haven't noticed, you little ingrate, *I'm* the one calling the shots. Get them out of there!" Sligo ordered over the speaker.

I sensed someone rush at us, and the force knocked me to the ground.

"Help!" Winter screamed. "Somebody help us!" But Winter's cries were quickly muffled.

I clawed at the earth in a futile attempt to hang onto something as I was grabbed from behind.

A thick, heavy hood was pulled over my face.

DAY 4

27 days to go . . .

Cenotaph
Memorial Park

12:21 am

"Get out of here," ordered a loud voice, waking me up with a jolt. My hands instinctively flew up to cover my head. "Come on, get up and get out."

A very serious-looking police officer glared down at me.

"Get your girlfriend on her feet and get out of here," she said. "This is not a place to camp for the night, do you hear me?"

I looked to my right at Winter. She was already scrambling to stand and began pulling me up. Her eyes were wild, and her hair looked matted with knots. Her knees were dirty and grazed.

"We're leaving now," she said.

Together we half-stumbled, half-ran out of the cenotaph, with no memory of how or when we'd been dumped there.

Winter's House
Dolphin Point

1:36 am

As we staggered towards Winter's place, all I could think about was Cal. Sligo had him in his clutches and was bent on revenge. How could I save my friend?

"You were right," I said to Winter, as we approached her house. "You knew Sligo was still alive."

But she wouldn't even look at me.

"I'm sorry I argued with you," I persisted. "I mean it."

"You *laughed* at me, Boges," she said, turning her tear-streaked face to mine. "You told me I was 'just paranoid' thinking there was a chance someone had made it out of the Inisrue Marsh alive."

"Like I said, I'm sorry."

"Whatever, it doesn't help Cal, now, does it?" she said, as she approached her front door. She unlocked it, threw it open, and stormed inside and up the stairs.

"Hey!" I called after her, taking the stairs two at a time. I ran to her room and flung the door open. I'd come up with a plan. "We have to work together to get Cal out of this. I have an idea."

Winter turned and glared at me.

I held up my hands, palms facing me. "Look at my nails."

"Boges, have you gone completely nuts?"

I shook my head. "Soil profiling," I said. "I have physical evidence under my fingernails. I'll scrape it out and find out what's in it."

Winter's anger and disappointment shifted. "You mean we could get some answers? About where we were taken? But how?"

"Different soils have different profiles depending on the areas they come from. It's not like pinpointing a position on a GPS, but it's a start!"

2:29 am

From one of Winter's kitchen drawers I found a small zip-lock bag. I pulled it out and headed for the bathroom. In the near-empty mirrored cabinets that sat above the marbled sink I found a metal nail file. I propped myself on the edge of the tub in the corner and carefully began scraping out the grit wedged under my fingernails into the bag.

My pathetic reflection glared at me from the corner of my eye. I turned my head left, facing it front-on. *Dude,* I thought to myself, *you look completely Neanderthal.* You belong in the Natural

History Museum, in a glass cabinet next to a pair of wooly mammoths. How could you have made it last with Maddy anyway?

I shook my bushy hair, and bits of grass and dirt rained down on the pristine tub. I scooped up some of it for my collection. I'd have to sneak into one of the school labs to analyze the soil and see if it would give me any clues as to where Sligo had taken us yesterday. If we managed to find that room, maybe we'd find something that would lead us to Cal's prison.

I knocked on Winter's bedroom door before walking in. She was sitting cross-legged at the head of her bed, a wool shawl wrapped around her shoulders. A small bedside lamp lit the room.

"There has to be something else in this," she said, without looking up. She was jabbing at Cal's coerced letter. "He was smart enough to get the *SLIGO* clue to us. There might be something else in here that we're missing."

I wanted to tell Winter not to get her hopes up—the letter was so short and written under Sligo's watchful, bulging *eye*. But the don't-you-dare look on her face warned me against it. I bit my tongue and sat down next to her.

"He took us to that hovel and showed us Cal, just to torture me," said Winter. "He didn't need to snatch us just to show us footage of Cal on a screen. He didn't need to, but he did. Just because he could. He's sick, Sligo."

She looked up at me with mascara-smudged eyes.

"We'll find him," I said. "We have to."

3:24 am

I couldn't sleep. I tossed and turned on the sofa, trying to get some rest.

Winter came thudding down the stairs.

I sat up. "What is it?" I called out, groping for the light switch.

"I've found something! I knew it!" she cried, jumping onto the sofa beside me. There was new hope in her voice.

"What is it?"

She held up Cal's letter. "Look at it," she said, holding it up in the light. "Notice anything unusual? The tiny smudges?"

"What smudges?" I said. I couldn't make out what she was talking about. I knew she wanted to believe there was another hidden clue in Cal's letter, but could that really be true?

I took the letter from her and held it close. I squinted at it and scanned the page for smudges until I understood.

She was right!

Dear Mum and Gab,

Sorry I took off without talking to you first.
Life has been tough lately. I'm not coping.
Gotta take a break for a while. Only a
few days or so to get some space from
all the attention.

Love Cal

There were six letters marked with a tiny, almost unnoticeable, smudge! I began reading them out loud. "C, O, F, F . . ." I stopped in amazement. "Coffin!" I shrieked. "He spelled out 'coffin'! Winter, have I told you you're the most amazing girl I've ever known?"

"Not lately."

"What do you think he's trying to tell us?" I wondered. "To go to the undertakers'?"

"Exactly! Someone *is* working with Sligo, we know that much. He has someone he's ordering around—helping him grab us from the clock tower. Whoever it was hiding in the shadows in that room we were in. What if Sheldrake Rathbone is alive, and Sligo lied about chucking his body in the bog? What if they're working together again? Rathbone's not exactly 'muscle,' but it sounds like he could be our man, and his brother's funeral parlor sounds like the perfect place to hide something."

I nodded, grabbing my jacket. "Call Ryan! Give him the address and tell him to meet us there. Let's go!"

Rathbone, Greaves and Diggory Temperance Lane

4:16 am

The three of us lurked in the dark of Temperance Lane, across the road from the undertakers' premises. It was just like last year, only now we had Ryan with us, not Cal.

"Check it out," Winter said, flicking her head

towards the storefront. "Looks like there's been a change in management."

She was right. The black-and-white sign that hung from the store roof over the sidewalk now read simply "Greaves and Diggory," like someone had painted over the "Rathbone" part.

I was nervous and starting to sweat. What if Cal wasn't in there? And if he *was* in there, who else were we going to come face to face with? Sligo? Rathbone? Or somebody else? Could we take them on? If only I'd had time to make up some more Disappearing Dust or bring some of my spyware to scope out the place first.

Winter looked fired up and ready for action, but I could see that Ryan was sweating like me.

"I almost fell on top of a dead person last time I was here," I told him.

"That had better not happen to me," said Ryan. "I love horror movies, but I wouldn't want to star in one."

Winter rolled her eyes. "The place seems deserted, but that's the way they'd want it to look." She patted her pocket where she'd stashed Cal's cryptic letter. "Let's go get him."

The three of us skulked silently across the road and along the side of the store.

Winter worked her magic on the back door and had it open in seconds.

I shuddered, thinking not only of the dead bodies we might find tucked away behind the jars of embalming fluid, but of Cal . . . and the poison coursing through his veins, slowly killing him. What if we were already too late?

The door opened slowly, and we crept inside, ready to attack. My heart was thumping rapidly in my chest.

Something was moving in the far corner. The three of us froze, not knowing what to do next.

As quietly as I could, I reached for the light switch on the wall. I glanced over at Winter's and Ryan's silhouettes beside me, then flicked it on.

Big black triangles suddenly swooped at us. Winter screamed and covered her head. Ryan and I ducked.

We slowly turned and watched as the pair of disturbed bats flew out the door and into the night.

I ran into the funeral parlor, now lit up and fully exposed.

Winter gasped. Ryan muttered. Aside from a broken broom propped up crookedly in the corner of the former showroom, the place had been completely stripped.

It was empty.

Cal wasn't there.

Infinity Gardens

9:12 am

Watchful black crows perched around us on white marble tombstones. I kicked at the dried-up flowers at my feet in frustration, and the crows flapped their wings and squawked in defiance.

After finding the funeral parlor empty, we'd gone straight to the cemetery where Cal had been buried alive. We'd searched it, completely blanketed it, but found no trace of Cal or Sligo there, either.

Winter pulled the letter out again. "Another dead end," she sighed. "Coffin, coffin, *coffin.* Cal," she said into the morning air, "what are you trying to tell us? Where *are* you?"

"We have no choice, we'll have to wait for Sligo to contact us again," said Ryan. "He won't hurt Cal. Not yet. He needs him alive so we'll do what he says. He wants money, right?" Ryan looked desperately at us both, willing us to agree.

I nodded, but didn't feel so sure that was all he would want.

"We can't just wait for Sligo," said Winter, looking up from the letter. "Cal put this message in here for us because he knew we'd figure it out. He knew we'd find him. We *can't* let him down."

"But maybe Ryan's right," I said. "You know

we can't go to the cops. That's not even an option. I can finish up the aerial drone I've been working on. Maybe it can help us keep an eye on this place while we're not here. Just in case we're missing something."

Ryan looked at me curiously.

"I've based the design on the Hummingbird Hawk-moth," I began.

"Another moth?" Winter interrupted. "Like the mothified listening bug Cal fired into Oriana de la Force's place?"

"Not quite the same, but similar. This one's *much* cooler. I'll thrill you with the details later. Besides, I've not quite finished it."

The three of us stared at each other silently for a moment. Then Ryan spoke quietly. "Don't the Ormonds have some kind of tomb or something, somewhere?"

Winter and I practically yelled in unison, "The Ormond mausoleum!"

"Genius!" I added, slapping Ryan on the back.

"Oh, but how do we get in?" said Winter. "I don't think we'll be able to get the key to the vault without making Mrs. Ormond suspicious."

"You're right," I reluctantly agreed. "She's suspicious already. We'll have to think of something else."

I pictured my room and all the surveillance

spies and half-finished inventions spread out on the floor. I knew exactly what *would* get inside that vault. "The Vipercam!" I said. "The Vipercam would be perfect! I've been working on something else that I think can—"

"Don't tell me," Ryan began, "you've invented some other robotic insect that can march miniscule explosives into locks?"

"Hey!" I laughed. "How did you know? I'm working on something exactly like that. But, nah, this one's more *reptilian*."

Ryan nodded at me, keen to hear more.

"The Vipercam is made up of tiny interconnected joints, like a snake," I explained, as we headed out of Infinity Gardens. "The joints help it worm along and infiltrate narrow passages. Its head—where the camera sits—is less than half an inch wide. It can weave its way through a crack in the stones and transmit footage to us while we wait outside."

"OK," said Winter dubiously. "Can this snake also see in the dark? And what about infiltrating *sealed* areas?" she added. "What if Cal's trapped in something . . . physically impenetrable?"

Like a coffin? I thought. "Not a problem. It has night vision and thermal infrared imaging. If anyone's in there, we'll find them."

"If there's anyone *alive* in there, you mean,"

she said solemnly.

I shrugged. When it came to Cal, I wasn't prepared to consider any other option.

Ormond Mausoleum
Crookwood Cemetery, Crookwood

11:19 am

"This place is creepy," whispered Ryan, shuddering as he gave the stony Ormond vault the once-over. The three of us were watching the vault from a few yards away, huddled behind a cold and crumbling tombstone. "All the mossy angels and cherubs . . . I'd be petrified in here at night."

I raised my eyebrows at Winter, as if to make sure she was noting I wasn't the only guy in the world to get spooked by graveyards. She smiled nervously at me.

Winter looked up and down the cemetery path, then when she was sure the coast was clear, she slipped over to the Ormond vault, her back against the closest wall. We quickly followed.

Ryan quietly crept around to the door and jangled the lock. He shook his head. Winter and I pressed our ears up to the rough stone of the wall. Nothing.

"Hey, Boges," said Winter, "what about this one?" She looked up at me from her crouched position in front of a thin, diagonal crack. "Wide enough?"

"Yep, that looks pretty good to me." I let my backpack fall to the ground and lifted the Vipercam out of its pouch like I was a real snake handler.

"Wow," said Ryan, ducking down to touch it. "That is unreal. Feels like real scales, too."

I eased it head-first into the gap, then activated it with my remote control. This wasn't your ordinary remote—it was complete with a touchpad and a multi-platform screen, showing plain sight, night vision and infrared. I flicked the touchpad gently, getting the device started. Inch by inch the viper wormed its way into the mausoleum, its black tail-end slowly disappearing into the crack.

The three of us huddled around the screen, hoping desperately for a sign of Cal, or some sort of clue. I took a deep breath as the inside of the mausoleum blinked into view, radiating in a slimy-green glow.

"We're looking for anything unusual—a flash of color, probably reddish," I explained, "that will tell us if there's something alive in there."

The Vipercam snaked its way around the vault. We watched anxiously, squinting at the green screen, begging for a sign of life. It covered a lot of ground, but the color of the screen did not change once. All we saw were the coffins on their shelves, dust and cobwebs. No one with a pulse had been in there for a long time.

"Sorry, guys," I said, finally admitting defeat. I sighed loudly. "He isn't here. This is not where Cal was telling us to go."

"There! Wait! What's that?" said Ryan, pointing to a small, kidney-shaped orange blur.

"Yeah, I see it too!" added Winter excitedly. "Boges, what's that?"

I tapped the screen twice on its position, zooming in on the shape.

The shape became clearer as it darted across the screen.

Ryan groaned when we realized what it was.

A rat.

We slumped against the mausoleum wall, defeated. I stared miserably at the remote as I slowly worked the Vipercam back out into the daylight.

The time and date at the bottom of the screen glared up at me. "Oh, no!" I cried.

Today was the day.

"What is it?" cried Winter, alarmed.

"I completely forgot."

"Forgot what, Boges?"

I sighed loudly. The most important date on my calendar, and I had totally forgotten it. "I was supposed to have my interview this morning," I paused, "with the NASA recruitment team."

Winter's face scrunched up. She knew how much this chance meant to me. "But can't you call them and apologize? Make another time?"

I shook my head. "They fly out this afternoon, back to the States. I've blown it. I've missed my chance."

My heart sank even further. I had let myself and my family down, and my best friend was still at the mercy of Vulkan Sligo.

DAY 9

22 days to go . . .

Home
Dorothy Road, Richmond

3:08 am

I woke up drenched in sweat from a nightmare. It was the same nightmare that I'd been having over and over again, ever since Cal disappeared.

I pushed the deadening disappointment about my missed chance with NASA to the back of my mind. I would just have to live with it. I'd fobbed off Mum about the interview. Told her they'd rescheduled. I couldn't admit to her that I'd stuffed up my once-in-a-lifetime chance.

Finding Cal was the most important thing right now.

I sat up and tore my blankets off me, panting in the bluish glow of my fish tank. *Another one*, I'd been warned in my dream. Another what? I took a few deep breaths.

Ahead, the smaller archerfish was roaming

the length of the tank like a prison guard. The bigger fish watched, hovering in the far corner.

Dude, chill out, I told myself. Cal will be OK. Sligo will call again, any moment now, and you'll do whatever he says, and then Cal will be returned, as good as new.

Simple.

Only we hadn't heard anything in days. I checked my phone, hoping for something from Winter . . . but nothing had changed. No one had called or texted me.

What was Sligo planning? What was taking him so long?

For now, all we could do was wait, but every day seemed to drag Cal further away from our grasp.

DAY 12

19 days to go . . .

Winter's House
Mansfield Way, Dolphin Point

1:56 pm

I was desperately trying to keep myself busy at Winter's place—anything to keep my mind off my nightmares and thoughts of Cal . . . but no matter what I did, I couldn't stop thinking about the fact that my best friend's life was in the hands of a monster. And that I couldn't work out Cal's "coffin" clue . . . and—my greatest fear—that the phone calls from Sligo had stopped because Cal was already dead.

I'd snuck into the school lab to check out the scrapings I'd collected from the room where Sligo had taken me and Winter. I used our lab's strongest light microscope, but when I saw the huge number of soil microbes, I knew I was beaten. They'd have to go to an expert.

I thought of Amy, an online friend of mine who was in her first year of college studying chemistry and forensic science. Maybe she could help me. I emailed her with a story about a non-existent science assignment on soil samples.

Winter pulled herself up onto the dining table—my makeshift workstation—next to my work in progress.

She rested her hands on her knees and frowned at the small, insect-like creature as she picked it up. "Boges, should I even ask what that is?" she said. Her hair dangled down to her thighs, wilder and longer than ever.

"That's my Hummingbird Hawk-moth. It has a tiny, battery-powered camera mounted here so it can transmit live footage," I said, showing her. "It's small enough not to get noticed. Its motor allows it to fly naturally, but even better than that, it can hover, like a tiny helicopter."

She put down the robotic insect. Normally, she'd have been full of questions.

"What's up?" I said. "Aside from the obvious," I added.

Winter took a deep breath.

"Talk to me," I said, prodding her leg with the tip of my tiny screwdriver. "You're making me nervous."

"Ryan just pulled up outside," she said. "I asked him to come over . . . the three of us need to talk."

I nodded slowly. She was right, enough was enough. I hated sitting around while Cal's life was at stake.

"We need to find a way of going to the cops without Sligo finding out," she said.

"Maybe an anonymous tip-off?" I suggested.

Ryan let himself in, and as he walked into the room, I flinched for a second—he looked so much like Cal. He went to speak, but before he could say anything, Winter's phone rang.

Anxiously we all leaned over her phone as it sat on the table in front of us.

Her fingers shook as she switched on the speaker.

"Miss me?" Sligo hissed. His voice sounded even creepier without the distortion. "How nice that I have all three of you together. Here's what you will do next."

"Where have you been? And how do you know we're all here? Are you watching us?" Winter cried. She jumped up and peered out the windows.

"We need to know that Cal's still OK," I said.

"Your friend is still alive," Sligo said flatly. "Just. That is all you need to know."

Ryan put his arm around Winter to calm her, but she shook him right off. "We're not doing anything for you until you put him on the phone!" she shouted.

"I already told you he would remain alive as long as you—"

"PUT HIM ON!"

"Well, because you asked so nicely, my dear, I'll make him squeal for you."

I gripped Winter's trembling hand as Sligo's voice was replaced by some muffled scraping sounds.

Finally, the line became clear again. We held our breath until we heard a whimpering sound.

"Cal? Is that you? Please say something," Winter begged. "Please!"

"Mum?" he finally whispered, his voice much softer and weaker than before.

"Cal, it's *Winter*! Are you—"

"Mum . . ." he moaned again, "where are you?"

We all cringed as we heard a pained shriek tear through the receiver. My heart raced with fear and horror at the thought of my best friend in the hands of this sadistic monster. What was Sligo doing to him?

"Now, here's what I want you to do," Sligo sneered.

"You pig!" Winter screamed. "What have you

done to him? You'd better not let him die! You said you wouldn't—"

"THAT'S ENOUGH!" ordered Sligo. "You heard his voice. He's alive. If you want him to stay that way, then you'd better shut your pretty little mouth and do as I say!"

Ryan wrapped his hand around Winter's mouth to silence her. She turned and collapsed into tears on his shoulder.

"Keep talking," I urged Sligo. "We're listening."

"The City Hall Charity Auction is coming up. I assume you know about it."

"Yes," I said. I knew exactly what he was talking about. The charity auction, to raise money for homeless kids, was just over two weeks away. Cal was *supposed* to be a guest of honor, donating one of Queen Elizabeth the First's jewels to the cause—a famous pendant featuring a gold phoenix. The pendant was valued at over ten million dollars because it was clearly visible in a famous painting of the queen. "If Cal doesn't turn up to that," I warned Sligo, "there'll be no more secrecy. And it won't be because of us. Everyone in the country will be looking for him."

"Our little deal will be well and truly sealed by then," purred Sligo. "Now, since I'm no longer on the City Hall Planning Committee . . ."

"Yeah, seeing as you're supposed to be dead and all," Ryan hissed.

I glared at Ryan. "We're listening," I said to Sligo again.

"As I was saying, I'm no longer on the committee, but that hasn't stopped me from making plans for the grand event. I want my presence to be known."

"But they think you're dead!" said Ryan. "And if you turn up you'll be arrested in seconds!"

"Oh, I know that," Sligo scoffed. "That's where *you* come in. You're going to arrange a viewing screen for center stage. In between the columns. I want *big*," he said, in a dramatic, lilting voice. "I want *impact*. I want to show *everyone* that I am back. I have something planned that will bring down the house!"

"Is that it?" I asked. "You'll let Cal go if we get you the screen?"

The uproarious laughter hurt my ears. It droned out of Winter's phone like a swarm of angry hornets.

"Will I let your little friend go for a TV screen?" mocked Sligo. "Ha! That's just the beginning. I have twenty million other demands waiting in line!"

"Twenty million?" I scoffed.

"Twenty million dollars, plus the Phoenix Pendant."

"The pendant? But that's crazy! That's the most valuable piece in the entire Ormond collection! And where are we going to get twenty million dollars from?"

"Crazy? I think not. Why should the Queen's little trinket go to some museum, when I could own it? And I am sure, Bodhan, that the Ormonds' finances, combined with the wealth of the Frey estate, should cover my financial needs rather comfortably. I will call again with details for the transfers."

"And then what?"

"When you've met my demands—not an inch or a penny less—I will release Cal on the night of the auction. So, get to work, and I will supply further instructions."

"Wait!" Winter cried. "What about the antidote?"

"Yes, of course, how careless of me. I will give Cal the antidote before I let him go."

After Sligo hung up we were left staring at each other in silence.

I buried my face in my hands. Cal's condition had severely deteriorated. He didn't sound like he had a clue about what was going on around him. How did we know he'd even make it until the night of the charity auction?

There was no reason on earth to trust Sligo.

My mind was reeling, processing the possibilities. Did Sligo really want to reveal himself to the world at this event? Show everyone that he was back—bigger and badder than ever?

"He's lying," said Winter. "That's not what he wants the screen for. He doesn't need us to organize that for him. Why can't he get his right-hand man to do that dirty work?"

"But what about the money?" Ryan asked. "He definitely needs us for that."

"Does he?" Winter asked. "Why couldn't he have kidnapped Cal and forced *him* to make the transfer of funds? He doesn't need us—*Cal* could have done that for him. Why keep Cal in a prison all this time? All Sligo has ever done is lie to us; what makes either of you think this time is any different?"

The glass coffee table cracked as Winter thumped it with her fist.

"Sligo's up to something far more sinister!" she said, her clenched fist trembling. "We have to find Cal before the night of the auction. We have to find him now. His life—and who knows what else—depends on it."

DAY 13

18 days to go . . .

9:10 am

Winter, Ryan and I spent most of the night trying to figure out what Sligo was really up to and arguing about whether or not to go to the cops.

But involving anyone else just seemed too risky . . .

We were on our own.

Afterwards, I'd drifted in and out of sleep, and in and out of nightmares. I'd been vaguely aware of Ryan creeping out of the living room to go home, but it was an incoming message on my phone that finally woke me up.

It was from Amy.

📱 boges, i ran your trace evidence. you are one mysterious dude . . . check your email.

I leapt over the cracked coffee table and ran to Winter's desk. I jumped on my laptop and opened my inbox.

Sure enough, there was Amy's email.

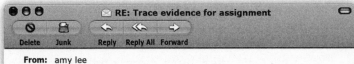

From: amy lee
To: bodhan michalko
Subject: RE: Trace evidence for assignment

Hey Boges

So I ran the samples you gave me and found mostly pretty standard stuff—common grasses, soil, grains of sand, things like that. But there was something in there that I couldn't identify, and had to take it to the palynologist. She was so excited when she found out what it was. Acacia pollen. *Acacia resurgere*, to be exact.

This particular species of acacia is exceptionally rare, so I don't have a clue how you collected your sample. It was rediscovered about a decade ago, after disappearing off the flora map for a long time. The flowers are a pale lemon color, dense and globular, approximately 1.5 centimeters in diameter. The leaves are mossy green with four to six glands lining the upper edge.

Are you testing me?

We've managed to track down four potential locations within this country—

Windsor
Castle Cove
Bowen Hill
Coffin Bay

Hope this helps. And I hope you explain to me one day what exactly you plan on doing with this data!

Ciao for now
Amy

I could hardly believe my eyes when I read the fourth location. My jaw dropped, my heart knocked at my ribs.

"Winter! Get over here now and take a look at this!"

Winter skidded up behind me, her white socks slipping on the tiles. I scooted my chair out of the way so she could read the email.

There was long moment of shocked silence. Then came Winter's elated voice. "*Coffin Bay!*" she shrieked.

"That's what Cal was trying to tell us," I said. I began looking up the location on my phone's GPS.

"Coffin! Coffin Bay!" she said, practically jumping up and down. "That's it! That's what he wanted us to find. Not the funeral parlor, not the graveyard, not the mausoleum, but a *place* called Coffin Bay!"

"That's where he is, all right," I added. I moved back in front of the computer and continued my map search. "Looks like Coffin Bay's a tiny inlet on the coast, about an hour and a half south." I hit "print" and turned to face Winter. "We'd better pack some stuff and get going!"

"I'll go call Ryan!" she said, running off.

"Cool," I said, jumping up, grabbing the printout and chucking my stuff into my bag. I checked to make sure I had my Vipercam and my new piece of work, the Hummingbird Hawk-moth, stashed securely inside.

Winter landed at the bottom of the stairs with a thud—she'd leapt from about five steps up. She pulled on a coat and slung her bag over her shoulder. "Ryan's on his way back over to pick us up now."

Coffin Bay

11:31 am

The drive seemed to take forever. The weather was bad, and Ryan had to crawl along with the windshield wipers going as fast as possible. Even then, the road kept disappearing in the blinding sheets of rain.

The rain eased just as Ryan parked the car a little way past the Coffin Bay road sign. We jumped out and looked down at the windswept coastline. Waves piled and crashed onto the deserted beach, and flecks of foam sprayed through the air.

We made our way down to the sand and across an outcrop of jagged rocks, leaning into the southerly wind that pushed against us as if resisting our intrusion on the tiny beach.

A cliff loomed on our right, and we kept close to it. The howling wind swept sand across the beach so hard it stung our ankles. Winter shook her hair from her face and tied it back in a tight braid. Ryan pulled his hood over his head and dug his hands into his pockets. I caught Winter glancing sideways at him. With his hair hidden, he looked just like Cal.

We stopped and scoped out the bay from a safe distance. I didn't want to walk into a trap like the last time.

But there wasn't a soul in sight.

"There's nothing here," said Ryan. "I don't see a building, a shed, a house . . . I don't see anything but sand and sea. Where could they be?"

"I don't know," said Winter, spinning around, scanning in all directions. "This has to be it," she said to herself. "*Coffin* Bay. This has to be what you were telling us, Cal."

A gust of wind picked up a clump of seaweed and threw it up into the air. We watched as it was swept up high above our heads, swirling the strong scent of salt around us.

Above us loomed a tall, craggy overhang. It marked the top of the cliff that reached a hundred yards into the sky.

"What about up there?" I suggested, pointing to the old sandstone lighthouse perched on its peak.

11:52 am

Carefully, we made our way up the side of the scrubby, sandy cliff, constantly scanning our surroundings, terrified someone was going to leap out of nowhere and pounce at any moment. Once we reached the top, we ducked down in the long, wet grass for a closer look.

We eyed the lighthouse carefully. It was about sixty feet tall and had a weather-beaten white lantern room on top. At its base were the ruins of what must have once been the keeper's quarters. Only a few blackened and crumbling sandstone bricks remained, marking out the rough layout of the original walls.

"Looks like a fire burned the cottage down," I whispered. "But it never reached the tower. Still, the lighthouse looks abandoned."

"Maybe," said Winter. "Or maybe it recently acquired a few new tenants. Follow me."

We crept through the grass and over to the lighthouse. The black wooden door was half-off its hinges.

Winter swiftly kicked the door. I dragged her back behind the sandstone wall as the door swung clear off its hinges and landed with a thud, sending up dust and sand. I held my breath for a second, half-expecting gunshots to ring out.

But after a minute or so of silence, I nodded

to Winter and Ryan, and we headed inside. The floor was covered in small black-and-white tiles, and a black spiral staircase curling around a thick white pylon led up to the lamp. The railing was bent and corroded from the sea air. It seemed like no one had set foot inside for a decade.

I started the climb first.

I had nothing but my fists to protect me when I emerged, a hundred steps later, into the lantern room.

But it too, was vacant. The windows were salt-smeared and cloudy, and the lamp itself was cracked and covered in cobwebs.

From the top of the lighthouse, overlooking Coffin Bay, we could follow the coastline for miles. The stormy sky still looked angry, but rays of sunshine were forging through. We looked down onto a flock of seagulls as they flew beneath, wheeling around the lantern.

"Look over here," said Winter, from the other side of the lamp. "What's this?"

Ryan and I walked around the perimeter to meet her. She was holding a small, worn, brown leather-covered book.

"It's a Bible," she said, flicking through the pages. A frayed ribbon dangled from the middle. "And look," Winter bent down and picked up a chipped red-and-white striped mug from the floor.

She tipped it upside down, and a small amount of liquid spilled out. "Tea?"

"So?" I replied.

"So, whose tea is this?"

"Could have been anyone's."

She thrust the book at me. "And this?"

I shrugged. It was just a Bible, sitting at the top of an old, abandoned lighthouse. Anyone could have been up here, trying to find some peace. It could have been sitting there, unopened, for years.

Winter squatted down and examined the floor of the lantern room. "Someone's been sitting here," she said, "recently. Look at the scuff marks in the dust."

I shrugged again. Dust was covering everything.

Winter glared at me, then shoved the leathery book into her bag, pushed past Ryan and rushed down the stairs.

12:16 pm

Strangely, the wind had died down, and an eerie stillness took over. I ran my hands through my hair.

Winter tentatively approached the edge of the cliff and peered over. She stood there, perilously close, staring out over the sea for ages, as if willing the wind to pick up again and carry her news of Cal. Not knowing where he was, not knowing how he was coping, was messing with our heads. But knowing that his nervous system was slowly shutting down and that he was on a timeline controlled by the unforgiving Vulkan Sligo was enough to send us all over the edge.

The wind suddenly swept up again, lifting Winter's hair. She stumbled forward, losing her footing. I lunged after her, grabbing her hand to pull her back. We listened to the echoing sound of stones tumbling and crashing onto the ground far below.

"That was close," she admitted nervously.

"Yeah, too close," I said. I stepped back and guided Winter away from the edge. "Whoa!" I yelled. The ground beneath my own feet was falling away!

I was stumbling, losing my balance . . . and before I knew it, I was airborne! Falling off the cliff!

"Boges!" Winter screamed.

This was it. I closed my eyes, waiting for my tumbling body to collide with the jagged rocks below. Everything blurred. And then something hit my back. I'd stopped falling.

"Boges!" Ryan yelled.

I opened my eyes and looked up. Ryan and

Winter were looking down on me from about forty feet up. Carefully, I peered around me. Some sort of scrubby tree had broken my fall. A scrubby tree with . . .

"Winter! Ryan!" I shouted.

"Oh, no, Boges, are you OK?" Winter cried desperately. "Please, tell me you haven't broken your back!"

I started laughing.

"Boges, this isn't funny," Winter pleaded.

"Look!" I shouted, pointing to a branch stretching out beside me. "Pale lemon flowers . . . mossy green leaves with glands. That's got to be the *Acacia resurgere*! We're close! We're close to where Sligo had us!"

1:07 pm

Winter hugged me tight and dragged me away from the cliff edge as soon as I was back on solid ground. Ryan had used a rope from the trunk of his car to help me get back up. It took us a while, but finding the acacia helped me forget about the danger I was in . . . and the bleeding cuts and scratches that lined my arms and legs.

"Hey!" Winter called suddenly, looking at something behind me. "Over there! Did you see that? I think I saw something move!"

Ryan and I turned around, but could only see grass, shifting in the breeze.

Winter started running, whipping her hands around in the greenery, trying to track down what she'd seen. *Was* there something here?

I untied the rope from around my waist, crawled to my shaky feet and joined her, swatting the grass.

1:33 pm

Eventually Winter stopped, letting herself fall to the ground in a heap. I looked over at Ryan. Despair was etched on his face.

I couldn't find anything either. I was fighting a growing feeling in my gut that the Coffin Bay breakthrough Amy had given us was going to end up as nothing but a coincidence and a false lead. We'd found the acacia, but there was no sign of Sligo here.

"OK, Hummingbird Hawk-moth," I said, as I lifted the gadget out of my bag, "time to do more than just hover around my bedroom." Using my remote, I gave the hawk-moth a short test flight to make sure it hadn't been crushed in my fall. It shot up into the air and circled on command.

"It's recording everything around and beneath it to a distance of seventy yards," I explained.

"Pretty good detail, too. But anything further than that gets a bit fuzzy."

If there's anything here worth finding, I told myself, the hawk-moth will find it.

DAY 14

17 days to go . . .

Winter's House
Mansfield Way, Dolphin Point

11:44 pm

"Hey, guys, get over here," said Ryan. I opened my eyes. We'd been taking shifts since yesterday, monitoring the footage from the hawk-moth, and I'd just fallen asleep on the rug on the floor. "I think I just saw something weird."

Winter leaned over him as he began rewinding the footage a few seconds. I jumped up to join them.

"Look!" he said, pointing at a dark shape on the screen that seemed to appear and then disappear up on the flat area behind the lighthouse, in the ruins of the keeper's quarters. "There—what was that?"

Ryan moved aside and let me take control. I rewound the footage and zoomed in on the moving object, adjusting the contrast to get some more definition. I hit "Play."

Again a dark figure appeared, then disappeared.

"That's a person, I'm sure of it," said Winter. "But it can't be Sligo. This person's too small. But where did they come from? The footage isn't skipping, is it?"

"Definitely not," I said, looking at the time code.

"It doesn't make sense," said Winter. "One second there's nothing, and the next—there's a figure crouched there. Like they've come out . . . from the ground."

I played the footage once more. This time it was clear. A dark figure seemed to materialize, crawling out of the ground. It looked up at the sky and glanced around like a meerkat, then quickly vanished once more.

"Underground?" said Ryan. "Did Sligo take you to an underground chamber? Like a bunker beneath the rubble of the lighthouse keeper's quarters?"

"Were we standing on top of it all along?" I wondered.

The three of us jumped up, wide-eyed, ready to roll again. The hawk-moth had given us the goods!

"Back to Coffin Bay!" I yelled.

DAY 15

16 days to go . . .

Coffin Bay

2:13 am

I stood in the darkness, straining to hear any-thing that might warn me of approaching danger. What if this was a setup? What if, instead of us watching Sligo, he was actually watching us, right now?

I jumped at the sound of a night bird's shriek and felt Winter tense up beside me.

"We have to be quiet. If they are here, we can't let them know we're on to them," Winter warned. "And if they heard us last time, they could be expecting us."

At night, the lighthouse looked ominous. Inside the ruins, Winter was on her hands and knees again, gently feeling around for some sort of inconsistency in the ground. I carefully kicked grass and stones around, looking for some sign of a dugout. We had flashlights with us, but didn't want to alert Sligo to our presence by lighting up our position, so we were counting on the moonlight to guide us.

Ryan seemed distracted. He kept looking around him. He'd been doing it since we'd left the car, down on the road by the neighboring beach.

"What's up?" I asked. "Think Sligo's watching us?"

"Nah, it's nothing. I'm probably just being paranoid."

"About what?" I persisted. Ryan was usually pretty cool, calm and collected, and right now he was rattled.

He gestured me forward with a subtle lift of his head, away from Winter. "I just had this feeling that someone was following us," he whispered. "I kept seeing this red car in the rearview mirror on the drive over here. I first noticed it behind us in Dolphin Point—when we'd stopped at some lights. Anyway, I didn't think anything more of it until I noticed it behind us again when we turned off the freeway."

"What are you guys whispering about?" asked Winter. "Come on, help me."

We turned our attention back to the ground.

"Hey," I said quietly, noticing something shiny in the grass. I reached out for it.

There was a metallic clicking noise, and "OWWW!" I shouted, falling in pain. Something had clamped down on my hand!

Ryan rushed over as Winter flicked on her flashlight and pointed it at me. Ryan gasped when he saw the jagged jaws of the bear trap crushing my left hand. Blood gushed from my torn flesh and dripped onto the ground.

"Careful," I cried, waving Winter away with my other hand, "there might be more." The pain was excruciating, but I tried to focus on rescuing Cal to stop myself from passing out.

"Ryan, quick! Help me get this off him," Winter begged. "You grab that side."

The pair pulled at opposite teeth of the jaws while I tried not to scream out in pain.

"It won't budge," said Winter. "We're going to have to try something else. Here," she said, pointing to a sandstone brick, "put your hand there, Boges."

"Why?" I moaned in agony.

"Just do it! We'll have to break it open," she said, picking up a piece of another brick and raising it above her head.

"No!" I said, but she was bringing the brick down fast. I shut my eyes. "OWW!"

An intense hit of pain rushed up my arm as the brick connected . . . but then the pressure released.

My hand was free. I hugged it close to me.

Ryan took off his sweater and pulled at my arm, wrapping my hand to stop the bleeding. Giant teeth marks sliced my skin in two neat lines. "Someone . . . clearly doesn't . . . want us here," I moaned.

I looked up, and Winter had a strange smirk on her face. I squinted at her, confused. She signaled down with her eyes.

I followed her gaze and the light from her flashlight and saw that the sandstone brick she'd picked up had revealed something underneath. Something small, round and rusty.

A small bronze ring.

She'd found a trapdoor. The lighthouse keeper *did* have an underground bunker!

"You OK?" she asked me. I gritted my teeth and nodded, pushing the pain out of my mind as much as I could.

Winter pulled the ring up, and before Ryan or I could say anything to stop her, she'd lifted the door and jumped down into the cavity below.

3:26 am

I jumped down next, followed quickly by Ryan. We dropped hard, about six feet to the floor. I cried out in pain as I rolled onto my injured hand. The trapdoor slammed shut above us, sealing us in darkness.

"This is where we were before!" Winter said, spinning around the dark room, shining her flashlight over the walls. "I'd remember this stench anywhere."

She was right. The room was about twelve feet square and smelled rank. The air was thick and hot, just like the last time we were here.

"Look at the TV," Winter added, panic rising in her voice. It was smashed to smithereens on the concrete floor. She kicked at it.

We all started feeling around the walls, searching for clues or hidden compartments. I found an old rope ladder hooked to a wall as I tried to ignore the throbbing pain in my hand.

"Do you think Cal was in here?" asked Ryan.

"Not sure," I said.

"No one's here now," said Winter. "What if we're too late?"

"No," I said flatly. This was *not* going to turn out to be another dead end. "Keep looking for clues. There must be something here that will lead us to Cal. Cover every square inch with your flashlights."

I sifted through what remained of the TV and held the end of the severed power cord under my flashlight. The wires were frayed, pulled forcefully from a socket. But where could there be an outlet down here?

3:39 am

I stood up, fighting off an overwhelming sense of defeat, and turned to my friends.

The hopelessness and exhaustion on their faces was undeniable.

Ryan wiped his forehead on his sleeve. "What do we do now?" he asked.

Just then, dust and dirt fell from the ceiling and rained down on us as the room trembled.

Someone was coming!

Instinctively, the three of us tensed and cowered, nervously looking up at the trapdoor.

Winter groaned. "What should we do?" she whispered. I could practically feel her heart thudding in the dank air between us.

"I don't know," I answered, scanning the space for an alternative escape route.

Ryan had his bulky flashlight raised above his head, ready to attack whoever was about to descend upon us.

The trapdoor creaked open.

"I thought I told him to leave the ladder out," a familiar voice muttered, as a hand fumbled inside the opening, pulling the rope ladder from the wall.

Sligo! That unmistakeable slimy, rasping voice!

We froze, not knowing what move to make next. We were trapped. He was coming through our only exit.

His bulbous body began squeezing down into the room. Moonlight seeped in through the small gaps as he climbed down. Luckily Sligo, wearing a ratty pinstriped suit, was facing away from us.

I held my breath and sensed the others doing so too. We would have just one chance to take him by surprise.

His gleaming black-and-white brogues landed with a thud, just in front of us. I backed away, silently herding Winter behind me, trying to ignore the pain in my injured hand.

Sligo groaned as he straightened up and grabbed his side with pain. He began. "I told you not to move the—"

His voice was cut off mid-sentence as a terrifying noise reverberated through the claustrophobic den.

"AAAARRGH!" Ryan screamed, as he charged Sligo like a vengeful bull. Sligo slammed up against the chamber wall.

"What have you done with my brother?" Ryan shouted. "Where is he?"

Sligo struggled to turn and meet his attacker. The right side of his face was pinned against the wall, and the left side of his dirt-streaked face shone with beads of sweat. His bulging eye, just visible behind Ryan, scanned the room frantically . . . until it found its target.

It locked onto something beside me and then froze there.

"Hello, Winter," he rasped, struggling under Ryan's grip. His bulging eye seemed to pulsate with wicked energy. "What a joy it is to see my former charge looking so desperate!"

I stepped further in front of my friend, protectively. I could sense her wanting to pounce, but I held my bandaged arm out to stop her.

"Ha!" laughed Sligo. "And so the trap catches the bear!"

"Shut up and tell us where Cal is," I said, putting my hand behind my back. "You need to do as *we* tell you now."

Sligo ignored me, intent on taunting Winter instead. "Aren't you going to say hello, sweetheart? Feeling lonely in that big old house of yours?" he sneered. "If you want company, I'm sure I can arrange someone to, ah, pop around and pay you a visit."

Ryan pushed him harder, and Sligo fell to his knees. Ryan lifted him back to his feet and shoved him up against the wall again, pinning him into position.

"Not so terrifying now, are you!" said Ryan.

Sligo was reaching out awkwardly for something on his left, but what? There was nothing in the room. It was empty.

But suddenly his fleshy fingers gripped a round, rocky protrusion in the wall, close to the corner. He pushed it flat with the palm of his hand, and it sank away. The wall on our left started moving. Like a huge stone sliding door! Were there two chambers down here?

Sligo dived through the opening, out of Ryan's startled grip.

Ryan and I flung ourselves on him, trying to pull him out. He mustn't get away!

But Sligo wasn't giving up. He kicked out, and I copped a hit square in the face and fell back, knocking Winter down with me.

As quickly as the opening had appeared, it began closing again. I swooped forward, shoving my bag in the gap to try to keep it wedged open.

Sligo kicked out at the bag and sent it flying, knocking flashlights everywhere. Zigzags of light fell to the floor with us.

"I'm losing him!" Ryan yelled, as his fingers slipped. "Boges, quick, help!"

Ryan desperately tried to hang onto Sligo's ankle, but it was too late. Sligo had disappeared behind the closing wall.

"Cal!" Winter was screaming. "Are you in there? We're here! We're here for you!"

I reached out, but the wall had already closed. Ryan was left clutching nothing but an empty shoe. He shook it, frustrated, then threw it hard against the wall on the other side of the room.

3:50 am

A piercing sound brought our attention up to the speaker in the corner. The three of us stared up at it, waiting for our next crippling message.

"Temper, temper," Sligo's voice mocked.

"Where's Cal?" Winter shouted. "What have you done with him?"

I ran my hand over the wall near the secret door, trying to find the protrusion Sligo had pushed to open it. But all I could find was a deep, round depression, as though the mechanism had jammed, or had sealed shut from the other side.

"There's no way we're leaving here without Cal," Winter cried. "Where is he?"

"No, you will not be leaving this chamber," Sligo warned. "If any of you make a move for the trapdoor, Cal dies. I don't want to end his life prematurely. Believe me, I don't. I have other plans for him first."

"What plans?" Winter shouted. "Plans for Cal? You said you'd give him the antidote and release him on the night of the charity auction!"

"Yes," Sligo said. "*If* you'd fulfilled your side of the deal, my little Delilah. But this changes everything. Very disappointing. How can I trust you now? Now that you've come spying on me? Maybe I should inject you *all* with a lethal dose of Toxillicide!"

"Toxillicide?" I repeated. He'd let the name of the poison slip. What was it? I'd never heard of it.

Winter nudged me urgently. "Boges, look," she whispered. "There's someone up there!" Moonlight streamed onto the floor. Someone had opened the trapdoor. And that someone was up there right now, listening to every word.

A bodyguard? Rathbone?

I braced myself for Sligo's accomplice to show himself. Instead, the moonlight vanished. Darkness fell as the trapdoor closed tightly again.

I jumped at the sound of Sligo shouting at someone. I couldn't make out what he was saying through the crackly speaker. Did he have someone in there with him?

A thought struck me. He was talking to Cal— he was right there on the other side of the wall! Had he been in there all along? I shone my flashlight on my friends' worried faces.

"We need to get into the other chamber!" I said, grabbing a piece of metal from the broken TV, jamming it into the tiny slit where the door had closed. I tried to use it like a crowbar, but it was no good. It bent under the pressure in seconds.

Ryan and Winter both grabbed with their fingers, trying to get a grip on the door.

"Whatever you're doing out there," Sligo roared, his voice deafening through the speaker, "stop immediately. Don't do something you'll regret! I'll kill him!"

I froze at these words and heard Winter's suppressed sob. But we had to do something to save our friend. I pressed the round depression in the wall nearby. Maybe if we could dismantle the mechanism, we might be able to get the wall to move again. But what could I use?

Suddenly I knew just what would do it. "Where's my bag?" I whispered.

"Here," said Winter, picking it up from the corner and handing it to me.

I swept my good hand through the pocket in the back, trying to find the tin capsule.

I pulled it out and cracked it open with my fingers. Out fell my latest toy. Unfinished, but that didn't matter right now.

"What's that? A beetle?" asked Ryan, shining his flashlight on it.

"Meet Atom Ant," I whispered. "It can't walk yet, but see its abdomen? Filled with explosives."

I placed the miniature grenade into the depression in the wall and pulled the tiny fangs out to activate it.

"Quick!" I said, grabbing my friends and pushing them down.

Winter's eyes widened in shock. "You're going to blow us all up!"

"Hope not." I tried to sound confident. "Cover your ears!"

The Ant exploded in a blinding flash, spraying us with minced concrete and rock.

Sligo yelled something from the other side of the wall, but I couldn't make it out.

I bolted over to the door and pulled back with everything I had. Ryan and Winter jumped up to help me, shaking dirt and debris from their hair. Shooting pains pulsed up my injured arm as inch by inch, the wall shifted.

"I'm warning you!" Sligo yelled.

Finally the door opened enough for us to see into the other, dimly-lit chamber.

Winter squeezed through the gap sideways and ran in.

I barely had time to register the size of the other chamber, except to notice it was twice as big as the dungeon we'd been held in. Trash littered the corners, there were two makeshift beds, dirty blankets, some buckets, shelves, dirty towels and a couple of lanterns. A tripod for the video camera, a desk, two widescreen laptops—one showing some type of architectural plans, the other flashing green like a sonar screen. And two red-and-white striped mugs, same as the one we'd seen at the lighthouse.

"Cal!" Winter screamed, skidding to a halt almost instantly.

I looked left. Cal lay slumped in Sligo's arms, hanging like a dead weight. Shocked, I saw the shackle that bolted his ankle to the stone wall.

But worse than that, Sligo held a syringe to Cal's neck, pressing it hard against his skin.

"Don't hurt him!" cried Winter.

"Then don't do anything stupid," Sligo warned. "Or come any closer. I *will* kill him."

Winter, Ryan and I backed up. I held my hands out, trying to calm Sligo.

"We won't," I said. "I promise. We won't do anything you don't want us to do. Just don't hurt Cal."

"Cal?" Winter whispered fearfully. "Talk to me! Say something!" Winter moved closer. Sligo thrust the needle harder against Cal's skin.

"OK, OK." Winter fell back, defeated.

"Cal!" I shouted. I needed to see him move, hear him speak.

The sight of my friend like this made me sick. I couldn't think.

Cal moaned. He was still alive!

Sligo adjusted his grip on Cal and scowled at us. Sweat dripped down his reddened cheeks and fell to the floor. "You'll wish you'd never come here!"

"No, Sligo, please!" Winter cried.

Sligo thrust the syringe towards Cal again, skimming his skin. "You want me to use this? Finish it right here and now?"

"Stop!" Winter pleaded. "Leave him alone! Let him go!"

"Why should I?" mocked Sligo. "I gave you very simple orders, and you have not obeyed them. What use is he to me anymore?"

Cal looked gray. My mind was whirling, but I couldn't think what to do.

The syringe's point began piercing Cal's skin.

"No!" Winter screamed, kicking herself free from Ryan, and charging, screaming, like a soldier going into battle. She hurled herself onto Sligo, knocking him off balance, and the two of them crashed to the ground.

Cal fell limply to the side.

"Cal! Winter!" I shouted, as Sligo rolled on top of Winter. "No!"

I couldn't lose my two best friends!

Where was the syringe?

Then both of them were suddenly, ominously, still.

Filled with dread, I helped Ryan grab Winter and lift her up, terrified at what we would find.

Her body was trembling and cold.

She was staring at Sligo, eyes wide with shock. Her breath was coming in short, sharp bursts. The syringe! Had Sligo stuck Winter with the lethal toxin?

I looked in her eyes. They were bloodshot and smudged with black. I desperately checked over her body, but couldn't find anything.

I turned to grab Sligo, then froze at what I saw.

The depressed syringe was sticking out of *his* chest!

He tried to pull himself up, but his knees gave way, and his body slowly slid down the wall. His legs kicked out in front of him, and he slumped to one side, eyes glassy, his movements heavy.

I shuffled Winter away from him as Ryan ran to Cal.

Sligo looked down at the syringe and up at Winter. He moaned. His eye bulged, streaming tears as it darted around the room haphazardly.

"It's OK," I whispered in her ear calmly. "It's OK."

The eye fixed on Winter. "We could have been an unstoppable team, you and me," Sligo gasped.

"Never," she panted. "I am nothing like you."

"I wanted it to be you," he said, grimacing with pain, "by my side. But you forced me to find someone else. My new . . . protégé . . . young, ambitious. He shows promise, just like you once did, Little Bird. The boy—"

The effort to speak was taking everything Sligo had. His body convulsed, then slumped like a severed puppet. I had to strain to hear his words.

"He's so fiendishly talented," Sligo whispered. "He knows so much . . . about botany, about electronics, about . . . *payback*. Perhaps he's even more wicked than I am."

"Who's he talking about?" Ryan asked, cradling Cal's head.

"I never planned on being stuck with you . . . after *the accident*," said Sligo, his whisper barely audible. "But you grew on me. You counted on me for everything. You needed me."

"I was ten years old. And you'd murdered my parents!" cried Winter.

"I wanted you there with me," continued Sligo, "but you had to go and ruin it, didn't you? You betrayed me . . . and you ran to the one boy capable of destroying everything I'd worked for."

Sligo's face was growing paler. Thin, purple-colored veins were pulsing across his temples, like parasites searching for a way out from under his skin.

"And here you are again . . . with Bodhan Michalko, the loyal best friend, and the Cal-clone, Ryan—or should I say, *Samuel*. I might not be able to show Cal's dying moments, but—"

"Cal's dying moments?" I yelled. "*That's* what you wanted the screen for! You were going to project Cal's death onto the big screen at City Hall!"

Sligo strained to lift his head to look at Cal. "He probably won't make it now anyway; I think I gave him too much . . . look at him. You didn't really think I'd let him live, did you?" Sligo laughed. His laughter turned into coughing. Flecks of saliva shot out of his mouth. "But it won't end here . . . I will still go out . . . with a bang!" he hissed.

"You're gone already," I jeered. "No one cares."

"And when the twin pillars of society descend," Sligo continued ominously, "the earth . . . will feel my power returning." Sligo held up a shaking fist and looked to the ceiling. "Everyone will remember me as the great hero who brought the house down! Still able to put on a great show for all the Philistines!"

Despite his fading powers, Sligo even managed an evil smirk.

"*What* is he raving about?" Ryan asked. "Great heroes and Philistines?"

"I don't know," I said. "I don't think *he* knows either."

Sligo's condition was worsening by the second, and so was Cal's. We had to find the antidote.

I scanned the shelves of the squalid chamber,

but all I could see was some jars of food and bottles of water. I ran to the jars, picking them up and checking their labels.

My search turned more desperate. We had to save Cal. We had to stop the poison!

I looked in the desk drawers and even through the papers on the floor.

Sligo half-laughed, half-coughed, bloody froth flying from his mouth.

"You'll never find it," he said.

"Where have you hidden it? Tell me! The lighthouse?" I hissed, lunging at him. Grabbing his collar, the panic inside me escalated to unimaginable heights. "Tell me!"

Vulkan Sligo's one good eye rolled back into his head.

Rallying the last of his strength, he spat in our faces. "You fools! You'll never find it. Because . . . because . . ."

I grabbed him around the throat.

Sligo choked out the last four words.

"There—is—no—antidote!"

4:25 am

Those terrible words smashed into my brain like sledgehammers. Disbelief took my breath away. I clutched at my chest.

Cal was barely breathing, and now I couldn't either. Everything was fading. Sound, light, feeling . . . the sight of Sligo's lifeless body . . . and Cal. There was no antidote. Our quest to find Cal had been for nothing. He was going to die anyway. Sligo had never intended him to live.

Ryan waved his hands in front of my face. "Come on, Boges, you're OK. Winter, get that trapdoor open—we need to get out of here."

"Cal will die," I moaned. My best friend lay as still as a corpse. "The Toxillicide . . . you heard Sligo. There's no antidote."

"Boges, snap out of it. We need you here." Ryan lifted me up and rested my head in between my knees.

I raised my head and saw Winter dabbing Cal's brow. She half-sobbed, half-whimpered, "Cal, it's me . . . Winter. We're here, Cal. We're all here for you." She wasn't leaving his side.

My strength and focus began returning as a cool breeze grazed my face. The trapdoor in the other chamber was opening . . .

The thud of someone's feet landing in the room next door forced me up. I swung my head around to the open wall.

"Who's there?" I shouted. Was it the mysterious accomplice?

A figure emerged.

"You? Willoughby? *You're* behind this! It was *you* on the surveillance footage!" I stumbled to my feet and ran at him, fists swinging. "You're the one who's been helping Sligo!"

"What?" he shouted, ducking away from me. "No! I haven't done anything but *help* you!"

"Help!" yelled Ryan.

"I've been following you," Willoughby said. "I knew something was seriously wrong when Cal disappeared. I could see it in your faces."

"You were in the red car following us!" Ryan yelled.

"Yes, that *was* me," he admitted, "but I have nothing to do with Sligo's plans. I was only doing my job, at first, chasing a story, but then it was obvious something big was going down. I trusted my journalistic instincts."

"Stuff your journalistic instincts," said Ryan. "Cal is dying!"

Winter sobbed on the ground, hugging Cal to her chest. She was whispering "sorry" over and over again, rocking back and forth.

"Look," said Willoughby. "I was here earlier. I heard Sligo say 'Toxillicide.' I've made some calls. Help is on the way."

"Great, he means the press is coming," said Ryan.

"I know Cal's story inside and out," the journalist continued, panting, "so when I knew what kind of trouble you were in, I ran and called—" Willoughby paused. "Can you let go of me?"

I took a step back, realizing I'd been holding him around his neck. "Called who?"

"Griff Kirby."

"What does Griff have to do with this?"

"He has connections to Dr. Leporello—an expert in toxins. I begged Kirby to pull in a favor. At first he told me he was out of the family business, that he'd turned his back on crime and wasn't going to bribe anyone for anything. But as soon as I mentioned Cal's name, he changed his mind. Told me he'd do anything for Cal Ormond."

Ryan looked at me questioningly. It *sounded* like the journalist was telling the truth.

"He said he'd get it and bring it here," Willoughby added. "He swore on his life. I don't know how long he'll be, but he's coming with the antidote." He peered around at Cal and Winter, then put his hand on my shoulder. "Cal's going to be OK."

7:18 am

"Griff, he's over here," I said, holding my hand

out for the antidote. "Quick! I don't know if he can hold on much longer!"

Griff had the syringe ready as he jumped down the last rungs of the rope ladder.

"Here, Leporello says it should kick in within five minutes."

Winter, Ryan and Ben watched nervously.

I took the syringe and pierced Cal's arm. I squeezed the plunger slowly, and the liquid disappeared into his bloodstream. We all held our breath.

Nothing happened.

Cal's face remained pale and lifeless.

Suddenly, Cal started coughing. White foam frothed from his lips.

Winter shrieked. "What's happening to him? We shouldn't have trusted Leporello! What if *he* made the Toxillicide for Sligo? What if we've just given Cal more poison!"

"He wouldn't," pleaded Griff. "He owes me. He would never double-cross me! There's no way!"

"Well, what's wrong with him?" Winter cried, helping me hold Cal upright. Cal started shaking violently. "He's worse! Look at him . . . we should have called an ambulance!"

"I—I—" Griff stuttered.

And then, just as suddenly, Cal was still again.

Slow, painstaking seconds ticked by . . . then Cal coughed and groggily lifted his head.

"What did I miss?" he murmured.

DAY 20

11 days to go . . .

Winter's House
Mansfield Way, Dolphin Point

11:02 pm

I woke up drenched in sweat from a nightmare.
Again.

"You OK?" Winter called out from the kitchen.

Dude, get a grip, I told myself again, sitting
up. Cal's OK. He's fine. You know where he is.
He's right there, resting. Recovering.

I looked over at him, sleeping on a foldout bed
just on the other side of the coffee table. He was
so much better already. As soon as the Toxillicide
antidote had started to work, we'd moved him to
Winter's house. Jennifer Smith, the nurse who'd
watched over Tom Ormond in the hospice before
he died, had taken time off from her research job
so she could help Cal through his recovery. She'd
been awesome.

We'd left Griff and Ben behind in Coffin Bay.

They were going to make an anonymous call to the police, alerting them to Sligo's hide-out. Lucky for Sligo, Leporello had made enough antidote for two doses. And no matter how evil Sligo was, neither Ben nor Griff were cold-blooded killers, so they'd injected him with the antidote before fleeing the hilltop to allow the cops to mop up the mess.

We convinced Mrs. O. that Cal was coming home soon, and that he just wanted one more week to get his head together. Unfortunately, Ryan and I still had to show our faces at the start of school. But we'd spent every spare second at Winter's place, willing Cal to recover.

Winter approached, and I shuffled over to make room for her on the couch. She sat down next to me, flicked on the lamp and gave me a glass of water. "Bad dreams, eh? Want to talk about it?"

I gulped down the water and recalled the images and words that had blazed through my sleep only moments ago. "It's stupid," I said with a laugh. "I feel like I'm Cal, dreaming about that white toy dog!"

"Don't feel stupid. You can't control what comes to you in your dreams. Sometimes they're helpful," she added thoughtfully.

"It's a weird nightmare I've been having ever

since Cal went missing," I said. "I don't understand why I'm still having this nightmare. Cal's back, and Sligo's in a coma in a secure hospital ward. Ben Willoughby's promised not to go public with the story, so long as Cal gives him that exclusive interview he promised him, and the police know nothing about us being in Coffin Bay . . ."

Winter shrugged. "Give it time. We've only had Cal back for a few days."

"It's like everything that happened to Cal last year is morphing into one big messed-up montage in *my* memories. There's stuff in there that he's only told me about. There are people and places I know, but have never seen before."

"Like . . ?"

"Like in one part, I'm in the Manresa Convent, where Cal tracked down his great-aunt Millicent, the nun. She's lying on this old bed, she's dying, I think. She's moaning, tossing and turning. She wants to tell me something, but her mouth is stitched up. Gross, right?"

Winter cringed in agreement.

"The corridor outside turns into a tunnel, and I feel like an out-of-control train's bearing down on us. I can hear the brakes screeching and the whistle screaming. Any second it's going to slam into us . . . I look down at Millicent, and her eyes have turned blood-red . . . the falling angel from the red wax seal is swirling around and around her pupils. The train's getting closer, I'm freaking out, Millicent's moaning, and then—"

"What, what?" Winter asks. She's watching me like a kid at a campfire.

"And then she speaks," I said. "The stitches tear away from her mouth, and she speaks."

"So what does she say?"

"She says, *There's another one! Another one!*"

I watched as Winter shuddered, shaking my dream away. "Another one? Another what?"

"You tell me."

"What are you two talking about?" Cal asked, lifting his head from the pillow.

"Dude, hey, how you feeling?"

"Not bad," he said softly. "Still feeling a bit groggy, but that's about it."

Winter hopped up from beside me and wandered over to Cal. "Can I get you anything? Water? Painkillers?"

"No, thanks, I'm good. Just tired."

"And how about me, Winter?" I asked. "I've been wounded too, you know," I teased, holding up my injured hand. "I know it's not like being mauled by a *lion* or anything, but still . . ."

"Oh, very funny. You'll be all right," said Winter. "And Cal, Repro and Griff are stopping by again in the morning, remember?"

"Yeah, yeah, that'll be good," Cal said.

"And Jen says you'll definitely be good to go home in about a week," Winter added.

"Sweet," said Cal, before drifting back to sleep again.

"Boges," whispered Winter, after a moment.

"Yeah?"

"I'm so relieved Cal's back," she said.

"Me, too."

"But . . . I feel like something's not quite right."

The darkness of my bad dream, and the disturbing warning of *another one* was keeping me from settling, too. I knew I'd be feeling better if Sligo was dead. And if there wasn't the mystery of his accomplice still looming in the air . . . but I bit my tongue.

"Like you said, Winter, it will just take time. I bet when Cal's back home next week, and we see Mrs. O. and Gab happy again, things will pick up where they left off. Who knows, we might even get to have that movie night after all."

DAY 29

2 days to go . . .

Mrs. Ormond took Cal's face gently in her hands. "Are you sure you're OK with me and Gab going tomorrow? I feel like you've only just come back from Melba's house, and now we're taking off on a glamorous cruise ship and leaving you behind!"

"Please, Mum," Cal replied, as though he'd been asked the same question a thousand times, which he probably had. "I want you both to go and have fun. I'm fine here, I promise. We can all hang out together when you get back. I promise. These guys will look after me until then."

Cal smirked at us knowingly. Winter, Ryan and I shuffled on the spot. Miraculously, we'd managed to keep the whole crazy Sligo incident under wraps . . . so far. Out of the press, and out of the Ormond household.

"What about the auction tomorrow night—are you sure you're up to it?" Mrs. Ormond added, still holding Cal's face in her hands. "It sounds like it's going to be a pretty big event. You don't have to go, you know. They'll understand."

"It's cool, Mum. Everyone's coming with me," he said, looking over at us again.

I grinned and nodded at Mrs. Ormond reassuringly.

"OK," she said, leaning in to kiss him on the forehead. "Goodnight, guys," she added, smiling at us. "Good luck tomorrow night, if I don't see you before we go."

"Have a great trip," I said.

Gabbi had been busy texting, sitting on the kitchen counter. She tucked her phone into her pocket, slid off the table to her feet and clomped over to us in her Ugg boots. She gave each of us a warm, sleepy hug.

"Night," she said. "Hope you guys enjoy school while I'm off on the cruise!" she laughed.

11:57 pm

"Here we go," I said, looking at my friends. Cal and Winter were sitting on my left, tucking into a bag of microwave popcorn, and Ryan was on my right, playing with the electric recliner button on his chair. He'd stretched it to its limits and was lying flat, at practically one-eighty degrees, facing the ceiling.

Almost a month had passed since we'd last

attempted our midnight screening in the home theater. And what a month it had been. But now, here we were, relaxing at last.

"Finally," I said, stretching and nuzzling into my deep, plush chair.

"Ooh, yeah," Ryan commented from flat on his back. "Hey, Boges," he said, sitting up a bit, "there are more chairs here, you know. Four, in fact. You should have asked Maddy over to join us."

"Mmm, yeah, maybe next time," I said. But I knew that was unlikely. I doubted Maddy would ever want to speak to me again after the weird way I'd been acting. I'd been too scared to talk to her at school.

All of a sudden my chair didn't feel so comfortable.

"Or maybe I'll ask *four* girls to come over," I scoffed. "Why limit myself to one?"

Ryan and Cal laughed. I glanced over at Winter, waiting for her to groan or throw something at me. But she was staring coldly ahead at the wide, blank screen, oblivious. Completely in her own world.

I noticed Cal craning his neck to look at Winter. He waved his hand in her line of sight, and she shook her head, turned and smiled at him.

"You OK?" he asked her softly.

"Absolutely," she said enthusiastically. "As long as you are," she added.

Cal tucked a strand of hair behind her ear, then offered her some of his blanket. I recognized it as one that had been around for years. A wool patchwork blanket in blue and white. I think Mrs. Ormond had knitted it.

I didn't know whether it was the shock of everything that had gone on in Coffin Bay, or something else, but Winter wasn't herself. She'd been really quiet, not like the feisty Winter Frey I'd come to love *and* hate. I'd given her plenty of golden opportunities to get me, and she hadn't taken up any of them.

I knew too well what it felt like to think I'd lost Cal; we'd both had to deal with that fear. And I knew Cal had become her family.

But it was none of those things. It was something different. Something lingering. Something I'd seen in her all year.

It was like she *still* didn't think it was over. Like she was *still* watching her back.

DAY 30

1 day to go . . .

12:00 am

"So what are we waiting for?" I asked, jiggling in my seat and looking at the huge white rectangle of light in front of us. "Let's get this vampire show on the road."

"Oh, the *Nosferatu* DVD. I think I might have taken it upstairs," said Cal.

Ryan jumped up. "Stay there, I'll go get it."

"That's OK. I *can* walk," Cal muttered.

"Yeah, yeah, I know, but I'm already up. No dramas. Where is it?"

"Somewhere near my bed, I think. Thanks, man."

While we waited for Ryan to come back, Cal held his hands up in the projector light, making claw-like shapes scratch across the screen.

I propped my hand up in the shape of a rabbit and made it hop about.

Cal laughed. His shadow claws promptly sliced through my lame rabbit.

"Arrgghhhh!" I shrieked, sending my rabbit tumbling off screen in slow motion. "Nooooo!"

"Ha, the show's already started," Ryan joked. He walked back into the room with the DVD and a creamy-colored envelope in his hand. "What's this?" he said to Cal, flinging him the envelope like a frisbee. "I found it on your pillow."

Winter leaned over Cal and snatched the envelope away from him. I hit the button on my chair and zoomed into an upright position.

Cal sat up. "Hey! Winter, what are you doing?"

Winter stood up and pulled the envelope clear out of Cal's reach. She stared at the paper intensely, her forehead forcing two perturbed chasms between her eyebrows. She turned the envelope over and gasped. "What?" I asked.

She held the back of it up to me, her big, dark eyes searching mine.

A red wax seal.

Pressed with a falling angel.

Another one.

"How did that get there?" I demanded.

"Give me that," snapped Cal. He flung his blanket off, hoisted himself out of his chair and snatched the envelope back from Winter. He went pale in seconds, making the bruises on his arms and legs stand out. The ones he'd been so careful to hide from his mum and sister. He shook his head as he stuffed the paper into his pocket.

"Cal," said Winter, taking his hand firmly.

"What?" He pulled his hand away. "Everyone's waiting for us. Come on, let's get the movie started already. It's after midnight. We've waited long enough."

"We know that's not the first one," said Winter, sneaking a glance at me. She grabbed her bag from the floor and began rifling through it. "When you disappeared, I found this." From a plastic pocket in her wallet she pulled out a matching red wax seal. "Cal, what's in there? What's going on? Please show us."

"No."

"Cal? You have to!"

"No," he insisted, "I don't have to do anything. It's nothing. Don't turn this into a big deal, please. We've all been through enough already."

"But—"

"Winter, you're always saying, *it's not over, it's not over* . . . you need to let it go!"

Fire burned in Winter's eyes. "And I've been right every time so far, haven't I?" She snatched the note from his pocket and tore it open.

I ran behind her to see what was inside.

Cal stood frozen on the spot.

"You OK?" I asked him. "Cal?"

He just glared at me, then at Winter, then Ryan. And then he turned and ran, bolting for the front door.

"Cal?" I called. We ran after him, into the cold night air.

"What does this mean, Cal?" Winter demanded. "What did the other note say?"

Cal stopped at the end of the driveway. His hands were clenched in frustration as he looked up and down the street.

"Talk to us," said Winter. "Please."

"Dude, what's going on?" I said, trying to sound calm.

Cal sat down on the pavement and took a deep breath. I sat beside him and threw my arm around his shoulder. Winter and Ryan stood together nearby, their tall shadows falling across our faces.

"Whatever it is, we can handle it," I said. "But you need to tell us what the other note said."

Cal exhaled loudly before speaking.

"It said '30 days.' I found it just before midnight when I was waiting for you guys. Twenty-nine days ago . . . on the night I disappeared."

He pulled at a blade of grass and began tearing it perfectly down the middle. "At first I thought it was a hoax—a media stunt, but then when I was shot with the tranquilizer dart and poisoned, I figured Sligo was behind it. But now . . . now I don't know what to think. I don't know why I have this countdown, or who's behind it."

"But Sligo's in a coma," said Ryan, stating the obvious.

Cal had hardly spoken of his time with Sligo. He said he barely remembered anything after he was shot in the thigh out in the front yard.

Winter was shaking her head.

"What?" said Cal, reaching up and taking Winter's hand.

"I just knew this wasn't over," she murmured.

"Sligo is in a coma. In a secure hospital ward," Cal said, now pulling himself together and trying to calm the situation.

"I know," said Winter defiantly. "He's out of action. But it's something else, guys. I mean it. I know you can feel it too, Cal. This is serious, this note. Sligo said he had someone working for him. What if this person is going to try to finish what he began?"

"But by doing what?" Cal pleaded.

This warning must have come from Sligo's accomplice. *One day*? I thought to myself. What was happening in the next twenty-four hours? What was this warning about?

"Tomorrow night!" shrieked Winter. "The charity auction!"

"What about it?" asked Ryan. "*Sligo* wanted us to set up the giant screen to show everyone he was back. *He* wanted to show Cal's . . . death," he added quietly, nervously looking at his twin. "But that's all over now. Ancient history. He can't do any of that."

My eyes locked on Cal's. Without speaking, I knew we were both on the same page. Something bad was going down at City Hall tomorrow night. Just what, none of us had figured out yet.

Winter's House
Mansfield Way, Dolphin Point

1:26 am

Ryan drove us over to Winter's house, where we didn't have to worry about waking up Mrs. Ormond and Gab, and where I could check up on what had happened to my Hummingbird Hawk-moth. In the crazy aftermath of tracking down Cal in Coffin Bay, I hadn't had the chance to recover it. I knew it would have stopped surveillance shortly after we left the bay, but now that I couldn't shake the image of the slight figure—so different from Sligo's bulk—crawling in and out of the underground chamber, I wanted to check if we had captured him again.

I scanned the footage at high speed, while Winter, Cal and Ryan watched on. I slowed it up when I recognized the three of us on top of the cliff and saw myself getting my arm caught in that trap. I winced at the memory. Then we saw our small, shadowy selves slip into the chamber, followed soon after by Sligo, who seemed to have come down the grassy hill to the north of the lighthouse.

The footage reminded me about the small Bible Winter found at the lighthouse. A few times I'd caught her leafing through it when she thought no one was looking.

"Hey, hey, wait," said Cal excitedly, interrupting my thoughts. "Who's that, there? That blur." He pointed to a small, grayish figure, slowly approaching the location of the trapdoor. It seemed to dart its head around, making sure the coast was clear.

"That's Willoughby," explained Winter, leaning forward and tapping the screen. "That's the moment he heard Sligo call out the name of the poison. See," she said, pointing to Willoughby's slight frame as he fled the scene, off to call Griff Kirby.

"Who knew Willoughby would save the day," said Ryan.

"Yeah, I never thought I'd be thanking that guy for coming into my life," said Cal. "Or Dr. Leporello!" he added, with an uncertain laugh.

I sped up the footage again until we saw Willoughby returning, then ourselves leaving, followed soon after by Ben and Griff. The flashing red and blue lights of the ambulance and police vehicles arrived not long after, courtesy of the anonymous phone call pinpointing the location of the supposedly deceased master criminal, Vulkan Sligo. And then the day emerged, and all was still again.

After zipping through a few more hours of footage, the picture cut out. The screen went totally blank.

"What happened?" said Cal. "Dead battery?"

"Not sure," I replied, rewinding the footage and slowing it down to play it again. "Nothing, nothing, nothing . . ." The unchanging scene unfolded again in slow motion. "There! What was that?"

"Looks like the hawk-moth flew into trouble," said Ryan.

I played it again, examining it frame by frame, until something big and black smashed onto the screen and then—blank.

"That's a rock or something," Ryan exclaimed. "Someone deliberately brought down your hawk-moth, Boges!"

3:23 am

"Coffee?" Winter offered.

"Yep, definitely." I stood up and ran my hands through my hair a few times. We were all so tired, but we had to work out what was going on. What did Sligo have in store for us tomorrow? Who was continuing to do his bidding, and why?

"But everyone else is dead," Cal called out over the hissing of the kettle. "Well, apart from Oriana—she's locked up. Hang on, what about Red Tank Top?"

That was pretty much what I'd asked myself when Cal first disappeared.

"That wasn't Red Tank Top who we saw creeping in and out of the chamber," said Winter. "I'd recognize his shape anywhere."

"Can we go over some of the stuff Sligo said in the chamber?" I suggested. "Maybe he let something slip. He said himself that he had someone 'young' working for him. Was there anything else?"

We mulled over the scene that had played out underground. Sligo was pretty messed up towards the end, and so was I, so I hadn't paid that much attention to what he was saying. I was intent on finding the antidote amongst Sligo's things. The antidote that hadn't existed until Dr. Leporello unexpectedly came to the rescue.

"Let's see," Ryan began. He rolled up the sleeves of his checkered shirt and folded his arms. "He said something like 'maybe I won't be able to show Cal dying.' And some sort of 'pillars of society' junk. Then what did he say?"

"But I'll still go out with a bang!" I said, suddenly remembering those words as clear as crystal. "That's it!" I said, jumping up in panic. "He said he wanted to bring the house down!"

"A *bomb!*" shouted Cal. "Sligo's going to blow up City Hall!"

4:00 am

Cal spoke slowly and calmly into his phone. He told the police we had reason to believe "someone" had set up a bomb inside City Hall, and that their bomb squad should search the place from top to bottom.

After quite some time, he hung up and returned to us.

"I think they made the Sligo connection, so they're taking it seriously," he said. "They've sent their bomb squad and specialist ops over there now to investigate."

Winter stood up and hugged Cal. She pulled back. "What are we supposed to do in the meantime?"

"Nothing," he said. "Just sit tight. Maybe we should all get some sleep. I doubt any of us will want to go to school tomorrow anyway. Winter, is it OK if we all crash down here tonight?"

"Sure, you guys can fight over the couches. I'll just go grab you some extra blankets."

5:07 am

Ryan's snoring hummed from the couch on my right, while Cal slept soundlessly on the left. I'd happily taken the floor of Winter's living room— I knew I wasn't going to sleep.

Even if the police cleared City Hall for the auction, and decked the place out with security and undercover officers, there was no way I was going, or letting my friends go, without being prepared. I crept away from the living room and headed for Winter's dining room table. I flicked on a lamp and rifled through my stuff.

Lately I'd been buying up bags of electronic supplies and outdated technology to see what I could refashion into something new and awesome. But right now, I was looking for earpieces and audio equipment. If Cal was going up on stage while the three of us watched from the audience below, I wanted audio in Cal's ear and a mouthpiece on his collar.

10:25 am

"Hey, you had any sleep at all?" Winter asked me, placing a warm hand on my shoulder and a mug of hot chocolate in front of me. I lifted my head—I must have fallen asleep. A pair of pliers was pressed into my cheek from where I'd slept on them. I peeled them off and cringed.

"Any news?" I looked around the room for Cal. Both living room couches were empty.

"Cal's just taken my bike and ducked home to see his mum and Gab off and to pick up his clothes for tonight. He'll be back this afternoon. Ryan's also gone to get some clothes and stuff. The police rang about fifteen minutes ago. They said the hall is secure. No trace of a bomb. They think the note is a hoax."

I raised my eyebrows.

"I know," said Winter. "I'm not convinced either. But they're monitoring the premises today. They're saying we'll be safe tonight, that everyone will be."

Sunlight was streaming in through the gaps in the blinds. I was going to have to go home to get my clothes, too. Winter picked up one of my earpieces and turned it over in her fingers. "What are these?" she said, skimming the table-top with her eyes. "There are four of them. Did you paint these to make them flesh colored?"

I nodded. "We're all wearing them tonight, if the auction's still going ahead. These, too." I emptied a small cardboard box, tipping out four silver swallows.

"What? My earrings! You separated the birds! What's with you fashioning my jewelry into covert communication pieces?"

"Sorry, but I needed something we could all wear as pins to function as mouthpieces, and you left these with your keys over by the door. Two earrings, four silver birds . . . one problem solved." I shrugged. I hoped she'd get over it.

"Promise me you'll ask first next time?" she sighed.

I held out my hand. "Let's count on there not being a next time."

Winter shook it. "Deal."

6:32 pm

Back home, Mum and Gran had looked at me like I was a stranger. I'd hardly spent any time with them lately. I hated disappointing them, but right now that seemed like all I could do. And all I could say to them was, "I'm sorry, I'll be home for dinner tomorrow, I promise," as I foraged through my wardrobe, looking for a decent shirt, tie and pants. They were dying to hear news about my NASA interview, and I knew I'd have to tell them the truth about it eventually. But not today.

In Winter's downstairs bathroom I threw on my clothes and realized I'd forgotten to grab some shoes.

Cal and Ryan looked cool. They were both wearing white shirts and thin ties. Cal's suit was black, Ryan's dark gray. Winter looked awesome. She was wearing an emerald-green strapless dress and white heels. Her hair fell in big curls over her shoulders.

I grinned at Cal, and he grinned back.

"Everyone wired up?" I asked, checking that my own swallow-pin mouthpiece and earpiece were working.

"Yep," everyone agreed.

"And we all know how to work these things?"

"Yep."

"Nice shoes," added Winter, checking out my white Converse sneakers. I struck a serious model pose in reply, turning and looking over my shoulder intensely, pouting my lips as far as they'd go.

"Pretty hot, right?"

Cal shook his head and smiled. "Let's get out of here," he said, shoving me.

City Hall

7:49 pm

Winter's leg jiggled nervously beside mine. Ryan was edgy, too. We were sitting at a round table close to the stage, waiting for the rest of the guests to arrive and take their seats. Cal was off with the museum curator, going over the night's proceedings. On our left, near the wall, stood a cop, decked out in black. He was like a statue, scanning the place with just a flick of his eyes. Opposite him, on the other side of the room like a mirror, stood another cop doing exactly the same. I'd counted six of them so far, placed strategically throughout the hall.

"I don't like this, Boges," whispered Winter. "I

feel like we're just waiting for something bad to happen." She opened her clutch bag and pulled out a packet of gum. Squeezed into her bag was that Bible again. "What?" she snapped, noticing me looking at it.

"You brought that ratty Bible with you?"

"Is that a problem, Boges? I feel like it could be important."

"Divine intervention?"

"That's not what it's about. I just have a feeling . . . that this belonged to Sligo," she said. "And that maybe there's something that we're missing."

"We're cool, Winter," I said, even though I was hating sitting still. "Just relax. Look at all the cops in here." I motioned with my eyes to the officers lining the walls.

"Something's not right." She tightened her hold on the small, fat Bible. "Every cell in my body is warning me."

I had to admit I agreed. I sat on the edge of my seat and looked around.

All the glass-topped tables in the hall were glowing purple from some sort of lighting underneath. In the center of each table stood tall glass cylinders filled with white flowers.

On the side of the stage, in front of the curtains, a string quartet played softly.

"Cal, how are you doing?" I whispered into my bird pin, perched on my collar.

"Hmm-hm," I heard in my earpiece. I reached into my waistband and turned the volume up on my receiver. I could hear someone talking to Cal about signaling when it was time for him to come on stage to present the Queen's pendant. He was supposed to step out, hand over the Phoenix Pendant in its velvet box, then everyone would ooh and ahh and clap, and he'd step off the stage and join us, taking the empty seat across the table.

Tons of other pieces had been donated for the auction, mostly artworks, antiques and sculptures. After the auction, there was going to be a formal five-course dinner, followed by some entertainment and dancing (no, thanks) into the early hours. We were in for a long night.

I turned around and looked at the faces filling the room. The city's richest and most influential people were gathering. The guy sitting on my left was some art expert who I was sure I'd seen in the paper before. He nodded at me, and I pulled my sneakers in tight under my chair.

I'd never seen so much sparkling bling, fur, freakishly white smiles, makeup, shiny suits and big hair in one place before. Some people I recognized—the mayor, council members, politicians, local celebrities, business tycoons, and a slick-looking guy who I suspected, from newspaper pictures I'd seen, was Murray "Toecutter" Durham's son. Anyone who was anyone was gathering here tonight. They stood in circles, laughing over crystal glasses of champagne. Oh, how Vulkan Sligo had wished to be one of them.

I thought of him, lying comatose in his hospital bed. He'd boasted about screening Cal's death and bringing the house down. I recalled his vengeful words. Of how he planned to go out with a . . .

Bang.

Sligo's threat would not leave my mind. The police had insisted they'd covered every inch of City Hall searching for explosives. They were thorough. There was nothing to worry about, right? The note sent to Cal was nothing but a coincidence.

A hoax and a coincidence.

If everything really was OK, then why was sweat building up on my forehead? And why did Winter look uneasier by the minute?

The lights dimmed, and the music stopped. A spotlight shone down on an old dude in a suit and bow tie, standing behind a podium. He cleared his throat.

"Welcome, distinguished guests, to this wonderful evening of art and altruism. I am Alistair Oates, the curator of the City Art Gallery and the co-founder of the Four Walls for the Children initiative."

Winter squirmed beside me. She looked as uncomfortable as I was feeling.

"Our guests of honor tonight are generous in innovation, intellect and spirit. They're the city's finest." He continued on, and I tuned out, on the lookout for trouble.

My gaze kept returning to something hovering high above us, some type of small, annoying insect.

Alistair introduced the guests. When Cal's name was spoken, the hall erupted into full-on applause. A few ladies in ball gowns even raised their perfectly manicured hands to their mouths and whooped for him.

I subtly ran my hands through my hair, leaned back in my chair and squinted up at the aggravating insect.

I nearly choked when I realized what it was. I bumped the table with my knee. The tall centerpiece vases rocked. I coughed as a distraction.

"Boges?" Winter whispered. "What's wrong?"

I pointed up to the aerial drone with my eyes. She looked at the ceiling, confused.

"The insect!" I hissed. "It's *my* Hummingbird Hawk-moth! Someone's using *my* surveillance scout to watch us!"

"The hawk-moth?" Winter repeated in disbelief. "We're being watched right now?"

"What's going on?" piped up Ryan, leaning over the table.

The woman sitting next to him glared at us. "Shh," she said, through a gash of red lipstick.

We sat back, rigid in our chairs. I was frantic, trying to figure out what this could mean. Who was controlling it, if not Sligo? Why were they watching us here?

"Boges," I heard Cal whisper in my earpiece. "What's going on? I can see you squirming out there. Everything OK?"

I couldn't answer. People were staring at me.

Back on stage, Alistair Whatever had finished his spiel, and the curtains were opening. The string quartet started up again.

On either side of the stage, two thick white pillars towered, just like the columns out in front of City Hall. The pillars began sinking into the stage flooring, slowly revealing two huge stone sculptures presented on top of them. As the sculptures, two ancient warriors standing guard, descended, everyone stared at them, bright-eyed.

Once they stood proudly positioned on the stage, the audience applauded.

"What are they?" I whispered to the guy on my left.

"Oh, aren't they exquisite?" he answered. "Apparently they arrived here just in the nick of time. Only about an hour ago! They're called 'The Twin Pillars of Society' by the sculptor Philippe Dioscuri. They're the reason I'm here tonight!"

Only arrived an hour ago? *Twin pillars?* Where had I heard that before?

My mind started spinning.

Sligo's words hit me like a head-on with a truck.

Twin pillars of society . . .

My power returning . . .

It was the sculptures! They'd arrived *after* the security sweep!

"Cal!" I whispered into my swallow pin. "The bomb! It's in one of the sculptures!"

"What?" he whispered back. "How do you know?"

"Shhhhh!" the woman with the red lipstick hissed.

"Boges, what's going on?" said Winter, gripping my arm firmly. Ryan leaned forward again, a worried look on his face.

I panicked. Before I even realized what I was doing, I was up and out of my chair. My body just took off before my brain had a chance to stop it!

I crash-landed onto the stage, ignoring the chaos I was causing around me.

"Cal!" I said into my pin. "The bomb! We have to stop it! Where are you?"

Cal ran out from backstage to join me, pushing and shoving other people out of his path.

"Boges!" I heard Winter shout from our table. "What on earth . . .?"

People looked stunned and stood up in shock. No one had any idea what I was doing.

Before anyone could stop me, I'd snatched up the auction hammer from the podium, dodged a gasping Alistair and swung at the first statue.

"Stop him!" people shouted. I ignored them. "Arrest that vandal!" someone yelled.

But I was already working my way down the body of the warrior statue, banging with my hammer. It sounded hollow. The hammer easily broke through. It wasn't marble, it was plaster!

Feet thundered towards me. The cops? A loud alarm sounded, throbbing through the hall.

"It's hollow!" I shouted to Cal. I stood back and with another big swing, I cracked the sculpture wide open and clawed inside the crumbling figure.

People shouted in horror and protest. Any second now I'd be grabbed by security. Inside the hollowed-out sculpture I saw exactly what we had feared.

Rectangular and mustard-colored. A blinking timer on top. A web of wires.

"Bomb!" I yelled at the top of my lungs. "Everyone out! There's a bomb!"

People screamed, running for the door. Cops dived at me, but I managed to scramble past them—the other sculpture was in my sights. What if it also harbored explosives? The nun's cries from my nightmares echoed in my head. *There's another one*, she'd said.

Another bomb? I had to get over there and check!

I pounced on the other sculpture. I swung the hammer in the exact same spot.

It was hollow too, and cracked open easily under the hammer. I pulled away the rocky casing and looked inside as a cop grabbed my legs and started dragging me away. I dropped the hammer, trying to get him off me.

"It's empty!" I shrieked, searching around me for Cal. "The other one's empty!"

But it had clearly been hollowed out—I didn't get it!

Winter and Ryan appeared on the stage, and they were staring into the second sculpture. Winter reached her hand in and felt around.

"Get the bomb squad back in here!" I heard a police officer yell.

Winter grabbed the auction hammer and swung at the guy who had my legs.

He screamed in pain, grabbing his back.

I dropped to the floor, legs freed. Cal and Ryan raced to help me up.

"The bomb," I panted, "in the first sculpture. It's on a timer! It's due to go off at . . ."

But I had another concern. I craned my neck, scanning the space above the last of the departing crowd, trying to track down my hawk-moth.

"What are you doing?" yelled Cal. "We have to get out of here!"

Now my friends were dragging me out.

"Look!" I said, pointing directly above me. "There it is! It's been turned against us."

They looked up at the hawk-moth.

"Who are you?!" I shouted at it.

"Come on, let's go!" said Winter.

I could hear sirens blaring outside. Finally, the place was completely clear of guests, and the bomb squad would be here in seconds. We ran out, dodging and leaping over toppled tables, abandoned coats, smashed glasses, plates and wine bottles.

We ran out the doors, into the dark and down the stony stairs of the building. And just before we reached the chaos that awaited us outside on the street—the flashing lights, the panicked, flustered, fleeing guests . . .

City Hall exploded.

In the nanosecond before I hit the ground, I saw the huge building split open against the night sky. Tall pillars, masonry, bricks and wood burst apart in the massive fireball.

The impact floored us. It slammed against our backs, forced us off our feet and propelled us into the air. We dived down and down and down . . .

8:27 pm

I opened my eyes.

I was sideways. Dirt, gravel, smoke and debris lined my vision. Beyond, the world was lit up by an evil light.

I couldn't hear anything but a thick buzzing.

I jerked my head up and looked down at my body. I was intact. My legs were OK; they were moving when I was telling them to.

But what about everyone else?

Shaking the thick fog from my mind, I crawled to my hands and knees. "Cal? Cal!"

"Boges," I heard him reply, "I'm here. I'm OK. You?"

"OK, I think," I said. "Where are the others?"

"I'm here," Winter's voice murmured.

"Here," added Ryan.

Slowly the warbling of ambulances and cop cars became louder again, and I found the strength to get up. I helped my friends to their feet. We were covered in dust, cuts and scratches, like we'd just stepped off a post-apocalyptic movie set.

"The hawk-moth," I said. "He set the bomb off early!"

"What do you mean, *early*?" Cal asked. "Who are you talking about?"

"The timer," I said, looking at my cracked watch and trying to ignore the ringing in my ears, "it was set to go off at midnight, when the party would have been in full swing. But someone was watching us."

"But who?" asked Winter, brushing gravel from her hair.

We scrambled over some of the debris, trying to see if anyone nearby was injured. Miraculously, we couldn't see anyone badly hurt, just people like us, whimpering and moaning, crawling to their feet, shocked and covered in gray dust. The four of us stumbled away from the wreck of City Hall and sought cover in a small park nearby.

"Cal! Winter!" someone called out, from the shadows of the trees. A familiar, lanky figure loped towards us. I'd recognize that green suit anywhere.

"Repro!" Winter called, jumping on him in a hug.

"Let me get my breath. It's a good thing you're all alive!" he puffed. "I remembered this was your big fancy night, Cal, and when I heard the explosion I knew it had to have something to do with you lot! So I came running! What happened? Are you all OK? All in one piece?" Repro looked us up and down, pulling and prodding here and there.

Cal covered his ears. "The ringing!" he said. "It won't stop!"

Ryan leaned towards Cal. "It's not your ears. It's your phone," he said.

Cal pulled his phone out of his jacket. A crack splintered across the glass screen.

"Who is it?" said Winter. She pulled the phone down so she could see the caller ID.

"No number," said Cal, squinting at his phone and rubbing the screen with his shirt.

"Put it on speaker," said Winter. "Quick!"

Cal answered the phone and switched on the speaker. He held it out for all of us to hear.

"I really didn't want to do that," the voice said, "but you gave me no choice."

"Who are you?" Cal demanded.

I stared at my friends, searching for recognition in their eyes. The caller sounded familiar somehow, but I couldn't work it out.

"My name is Elijah Smith, and before you put him in a coma in Coffin Bay, Vulkan Sligo taught me a thing or two about revenge."

Repro's possum eyes were bewildered, shining huge in the moonlight. He looked at us as if to say, *What's happening now?*

"Revenge?" I whispered to Winter, beside me. "Who is this guy? He sounds like he's just a kid!"

"Either way," whispered Winter, looking back at the smoking wreck of City Hall, "he's deadly serious."

Cal's hand shook as he held the phone. "I've never heard of you, Elijah," he said. "I don't know what you want with me."

"We know there's another bomb," I interrupted. "We saw inside the second sculpture. The second 'twin.' It was hollow too, but it was empty. The Semtex bomb had been removed." Everyone looked at me, questioningly. "What have you done with it? Where have you taken the bomb?"

"Sligo warned me about you, Boges," Elijah said simply. "You know your explosives, and you know how to craft a pretty handy aerial drone. I like your style. But I am also good with explosives, electronics . . . *and* toxins."

Cal was shaking his head. "Who are you?" he shouted. Cal's face was white despite the huge fire behind us.

"I told you, I'm Elijah Smith."

"Your name means nothing to me. Why are you hounding me? You don't need to take down City Hall to catch me!"

The phone line crackled, distorting Elijah's words. But one word came out clearly: *family.*

"Family? What are you talking about?" Cal asked. "You want a stake in the Ormond fortune? Get in line!"

The kid scoffed. "I don't care for money," he said. "I want *revenge.* It's *you* I want to destroy, Cal. You took all I had left, and now it's time for me to take something back."

"I don't get it! Take back what? If you want me, I'm right here," cried Cal, "outside City Hall. Where have you taken the other bomb?"

"Sligo was the one who wanted the world to witness your slow, pathetic death on the big screen. He was the one who wanted to—" the monotone voice paused, dramatically, "shake the columns of the palace."

"The palace?" Winter repeated. "City Hall?"

"I'm after something else," continued Elijah. "I know how to really make you suffer . . . I gave you thirty days to sweat on it."

"What?" said Cal, trying desperately to control his voice. "Thirty days? *You* sent me the note? What are you going to do?"

"You'll soon find out," said Elijah. "My only word of advice, Cal Ormond, before I go and *finish* this . . ."

Cal clenched the phone hard. "Is what?"

A rumbling noise started on the line as Elijah spoke again, ". . . is that at midnight tonight you had better watch out for one big *supernova*."

The phone line went dead.

"Supernova?" I repeated. "An exploding star? That doesn't make any sense!"

Cal's eyes widened. I heard his sharp intake of breath. "Exploding star?" he repeated.

"Do you know what he means?" I asked him.

Cal's face creased in agony. "*No*," he cried. "It can't be! He couldn't! But why?"

"What, Cal? If you know something, tell us! We don't have much time before midnight when that second bomb will go off—wherever it is!"

"He doesn't care about taking down City Hall!" Cal said.

"Dude, if you know where he is, we have to go there now!"

"He's talking about the *Star*!" cried Cal. "The cruise ship—the *Sapphire Star*. The second bomb is on the cruise ship! He wants to kill Mum and Gab!"

8:46 pm

"But it's miles out to sea already!" I said. I checked my watch and tried to run the calculations in my head, estimating the rough position of the ship. "No speedboat is going to get us there fast enough! The twin bomb is set to go off at midnight. We only have just over three hours to get out to sea, find the *Sapphire Star*, track down the bomb and diffuse it!"

"But the *Sapphire Star* is enormous!" said Repro, spreading his arms high and wide.

"But who is this guy, and why is he doing this to us?" Cal cried.

Winter was on her feet and running. "That doesn't matter right now. Come on!" she shouted to us. "I know something that will get us there in time. But we gotta run, come on!"

9:11 pm

Repro's fingers moved almost in a blur as he worked on the locks that were keeping the iron gates clamped shut. Old corrugated iron fencing surrounded the vast perimeter. What was Winter leading us to? I checked my watch. Two hours, forty-nine minutes to go.

As Repro hunched over, muttering incoherently, he clutched some sort of thin silver instrument that he worked back and forth at precise angles until we heard the click of the lock releasing. Ryan, Cal and I helped Repro pull the creaking gates open. Winter forced her way through the gap as soon as the opening was wide enough to take her.

"I hope you know what you're doing, Winter," said Cal.

"Trust me," she called back, without turning. "Hurry up, we need to get over there," she said. She pointed to a dark silhouette in the distance— a huge, wooden shed, bolted shut with more thick chains. Repro cracked his fingers wickedly as he loped along beside me. But as we approached the doors, Winter ran left and around the back of the building.

"Follow me," she called out.

As she turned the corner, I heard her exclaim, "Where's the other one gone?"

When I caught up and reached the clearing beyond the shed I stopped and stared. I could hardly believe what I was seeing, sitting on a green and brown sea of wild grasses.

A helicopter.

A black helicopter, quite a few years old, I guessed. Down its side, shining in the moonlight, read the words *Little Bird 2*. We must have been on one of the Frey properties that had been returned to Winter.

To the right of the helicopter, the grass was flat in two thick lines, like another one had been sitting there until not long ago.

I scanned my eyes over the blades, the fuselage, the skids. It reminded me of a rescue helicopter simulator I'd been practicing in after Cal and I had taken up an offer of free helicopter lessons a couple of months ago.

"Look, I know I've flown a plane before," said Cal, "and I've had a bit of helicopter training, with Boges, but maybe you're forgetting the fact that I crashed the Ormond Orca!"

Winter looked at me, eyebrows raised and hopeful. "But you've both had training!"

"Yeah, but we've never flown a *real* helicopter ourselves!" I interrupted. "We've always had a pilot beside us. I've flown remote-controlled choppers, and I've played around in a simulator, but this? This is way more complicated!"

"Repro?" she asked, impatiently moving her desperate gaze around the circle.

"Safe-cracker, martial artist, avid reader and collector, yes. Helicopter pilot? Certainly not!"

"Don't look at me," said Ryan, before Winter could ask him.

I looked at my watch again. We'd lost another five minutes. We had no more time to waste. My friends were a mess. Cal's eyes were glassy, his shirt was dripping in sweat. He was panting as he looked at me, desperately, for a solution.

Mrs. O. and Gab were in serious danger. They were under threat from someone Sligo had called more wicked than himself.

My mind frantically scanned my memory for all that simulator practice and the six flight lessons Cal and I had taken at the airfield.

I took a big gulp. "Come on, Cal," I said, charging towards the aircraft with a massive lump in my throat. "How hard can it be?"

9:28 pm

The rotors roared, whipping and flattening the grass around us like we were in the center of an enormous crop circle. There was no time for pre-flight checks as Cal and I stared at the controls, hands trembling as we tentatively prepared to take off. Neither of us wanted to be the first to try anything, but Cal finally plucked up the courage and got us moving. As we started lifting off the ground, my stomach lurched, and a sheet of corrugated iron ripped off the nearby shed and flew into the air, as if snatched by a violent cyclone.

I glanced at my friends. They all looked as terrified as I felt. I took control of the cyclic stick as Cal watched my every move from his seat on my right, helping as much as he could with the instruments. Winter and Repro looked at each other anxiously. Winter leaned forward and clasped Cal's shoulder. "We'll make it," she told him. "I promise."

Was that a promise *I* could keep? I gulped again, reaching for the collective lever and scanning the controls for what move I should make next. I was taunted by the thought of a petrifying plunge into the dark ocean, our screams echoing into the dark and empty night.

"Here we go!"

Like a drunken dragonfly, shaky and unsure, we took off into the sky and headed for the coast.

10:14 pm

The lights of the *Sapphire Star* were like a beacon, signaling us toward it, but we knew it was also sending us a deadly warning.

"It's huge," said Cal. "I've never seen anything like it."

"Me, neither," Repro added, his hands pressed up against the chopper glass. "It's lit up like a sideways skyscraper. I read that the *Sapphire Star* can carry almost ten thousand people. It's three hundred feet tall, and four hundred and fifty yards long. It has over twenty guest decks! You would not believe the stuff they have on this ship," Repro said excitedly. "Eight swimming pools, nightclubs, bowling alleys, dozens of bars and spas . . . and tonight there's some big Opening Gala in the Archipelago Arena. It's surrounded by an eighteen-foot-tall coral reef aquarium wall—filled with all kinds of blue-colored fish!"

"Eighteen-foot-tall aquarium? I thought my fish tank was big," I said, laughing nervously.

"It's rumored there's even a blue-ringed octopus in there," he added.

"The Archipelago Arena," Cal repeated. "I know Mum and Gab said something about a guest party at an aquarium . . . that must be it. I reckon that's where we'll find Elijah."

We were nearing the ship from the stern, and it was ridiculously massive. The width of the churning water left in its wake was huge, trailing for miles.

"What do we do now?" Ryan asked. "We can't land this thing on the ship."

Repro and Winter started digging around old equipment on the floor, trying to find some sort of winch that could possibly lower us onto the glowing ship.

"Here," said Repro, tapping a black panel near his leg. "A hoist. This is the operation control."

"Boges, can you get us close enough for me to drop down on this rope?" Cal asked.

"You're not going down there on your own," I said. "I'm coming, too."

"Boges, you can't come," said Winter. "We need you to look after this," she said, nodding up towards the thunderous rotor blades. "Like Ryan says, it's not like we can park it."

"I'll look after it, I've been watching Boges," said Repro, cracking his knuckles. "Yes," he added, nodding, "I'm pretty certain I can keep it under control."

I quickly studied Repro's face. He looked fearless and proud. And crazy enough to try to fly a helicopter.

At almost the highest point of the ship I saw a gleaming swimming pool on top of a tower, surrounded by a sun deck.

"We'll have to jump from the rope." I pointed down to the pool. "And that's where we're going to land."

10:21 pm

Cal shook Repro's hand as he took the controls, and we gave him a quick rundown of the blinking lights in the cockpit.

We crouched on the edge of the helicopter, each of us silently willing ourselves to do this. For Gabbi and Mrs. O. We couldn't fail them now.

Cal tentatively eased out of the chopper,

swinging out on the winch rope first. He swung for a moment longer . . . then let go and landed in the middle of the pool with an enormous splash.

One down, three to go. The wind from the rotors whipped around us as Ryan, Winter and I nervously took turns sliding down the winch rope a couple of yards and leaping off into the pool, following Cal.

My heart was pounding as I sank into the clear warm water, tucking my legs up beneath me, begging myself not to crack my head or my spine on the bottom. Finally I slowed, and my feet found the silky-smooth, tiled pool floor. I pushed off with as much force as possible and shot up to the surface.

I broke through it and gasped, sucking in air. Cal, Winter and Ryan burst up around me, sending sprays of water up in three arcs. A couple of swimmers by the pool's edge watched us in shock—the people who'd seemed to fall from the sky.

"Hey!" Voices boomed nearby. Three guys in white uniforms jogged across the pool deck, eyes to the sky. "What's that helicopter doing up there? That's the second one that's come over us in less than an hour!"

The chopper dipped, and the rotors roared

and sliced dangerously close to the ship. The water around us rippled like a wave machine.

"Repro!" Winter hissed. "He's losing control. He's going to crash!"

The chopper dived once more, disappearing down the side of the massive ship and out of sight.

Repro!

I swam beside Cal to the side of the pool and clambered out. We searched the skies for Repro. Our hearts thundered in time with the rotor blades.

And then the chopper rose again in the distance, swinging wildly.

"I hope he makes it back to shore," Cal whispered. He grabbed my shoulder. "But we have to go, Boges. We have to get down to the Arena!"

Around us were groups of people, laughing, sipping cocktails. Everything looked shiny and new. Soft blue lighting shone along the decks. I looked down and saw the words *Sapphire Star* glowing from the bottom of the pool.

"Follow me," Winter called from the water. "We have to get all the way to the other end of the ship, and I think I've just found a fast way there!"

She swam to the far side of the pool facing the center of the ship and pointed to a dip that seemed to lead over the edge, like a waterfall.

And just like that, she swam over it and vanished from sight.

With the guards closing in on us, Cal wasted no time jumping in and disappearing after her. Ryan looked at me and shrugged.

Bravely we dived in again and followed.

I held my breath as I found myself falling, then being splashed and funneled along in some sort of transparent neon tube. My body was careening along on a wave, looping around left and right.

We were soaring down a water slide!

"Woooooooooah!" Ryan yelled, coming down behind me.

Ahead, Winter and Cal's silhouettes slipped left and right along the curves of the tube.

I stretched back and shut my eyes, trying to relax into the ride, but quickly regretted it. Suddenly I felt sick in the wild spin. Out of nowhere, Rafe's face as he died, crushed under the Ormond Angel in Ireland, taunted me from behind my closed eyelids . . .

The four of us were flung out, airborne, and landed in another, larger pool on a lower deck. This time people nearby raised their glasses and cheered. I pushed my hair back and looked around. People in a mix of suits and gowns and bathing suits danced around the pool and the adjacent bubbling spas. Music was pumping at full volume. I tried to shake Rafe out of my mind. Why was I thinking about him at a time like this?

I followed Cal, Winter and Ryan and heaved myself out of the second pool and ran over to the railing. Beyond was a vast open space, the size of a football field, leading down into the many levels of guest cabins. We still had a long way to go. Thick wire cables led down from the pool deck to unseen depths of the ship. At the top of the four lines hung these harness-like ropes and cords, hooked into place, ready and waiting to go.

I looked at a sign in front of me.

I'd found our next way down. "Everyone ready to fly again?" I asked. "Follow me!"

I gripped the railing and hoisted myself over it, straddling it carefully.

"Grab one of these," I said. I unhooked the harness on the far left and clipped it around me. My clothes dripped all over the wooden planks at my feet.

"And then what?" said Ryan.

"And then hold on tight!" I said, launching off the railing and down the zip line.

The wind rushed at my face as I gathered speed. Blurs of onlookers pointing and watching my wild flying fox ride zoomed past me.

I looked back to check on my friends, carefully taking my weight into my right hand, and saw them coming after me. Winter's hair was whipping darkly behind her, blocking my view of Cal. Ryan had his legs flung out wide and was swinging side to side.

The end of the zip line was coming up fast. I slowed down completely, and then my feet were on solid ground again.

Winter, Cal and Ryan landed softly behind me.

10:51 pm

"Whoa, that was fast!" said Ryan. But then he frowned, abruptly remembering why we were there.

To stop a bomb. To save Gabbi and Mrs. Ormond.

To save ten thousand people. And we had only sixty-nine minutes to work out how.

"So where do we go next?" Ryan asked.

"I reckon Elijah's set up the bomb in the middle of the Gala," said Cal. "The party will be in full swing right now, and that's where most of the passengers will be. Including Mum and Gab."

Winter nodded. She pulled her hair back, twisting it with her hands, and wrung it out. "I agree," she said. "Let's try our best to fit in along the way, shall we?"

We walked along a corridor and stopped at a landing. Gold-flecked marble spread wide around us, leading perfectly symmetrically on both sides to what I guessed were the luxury suites. Cabin crew in stark white uniforms worked their way down the aisles, past gold-numbered doors, with silver trolleys topped with those fancy plate domes. Directly ahead was a grand staircase that split in two, curving around and down to the levels below in a love-heart shape.

"Where's the Gala?" Cal asked a passing crew member. "The Arena?"

The guy looked startled and peered at Cal curiously. He smoothed his neat goatee and slowly registered who was standing—still dripping—in front of him. He then stared at the rest of us, looking us up and down with a quick flick of his eyes, and smiled enthusiastically.

"We're running really late, meeting some friends," Cal explained.

"Of course. I will take you," he said, with what I guessed was a hint of a French accent. "I did not know you were aboard, Mr. Ormond. Please wait just one moment."

With a few quick steps he slipped out of sight, then returned with an armful of plush white towels.

"For you," he said, holding out a towel to Winter. "And sirs," he added, handing the rest to Cal, Ryan and me.

We grabbed the towels and dried off quickly.

The cabin steward spun around and hurriedly made his way down the right side of the staircase. He kept looking back at us, as though checking we were still there. "To the bow," he directed.

We followed him alongside a seamless golden banister that stretched past endless rooms and overlooked multiple restaurant decks. Everything about this ship was huge and expensive. I started calculating the figures in my mind, but gave up after about ten seconds. The extravagant marble columns, the crystal chandeliers, the blue glass lanterns that gave the air an azure glow . . . the perfect white tabletop linens, the mirror-clear cutlery—everything was spotless.

The shock of the City Hall explosion suddenly returned to me. My chest tightened. Everywhere I looked suddenly transformed into a war zone. Dust, debris, shattered glass, people wailing . . . a sinking ship.

Cal almost tripped as we walked along.

"Feeling all right?" I asked.

"Yep," he nodded. "We just need to find this guy already. We're running out of time."

There was no sign of the crew decks or the engine room, or the control room . . . I just hoped we were heading for the right place. There would be no time for backtracking if the bomb wasn't where we were expecting it to be.

"Here we are," announced the steward, as we turned a corner. He stopped and twisted, with a flourish, on his shiny shoes.

11:01 pm

The sound of thousands of people dancing, laughing, talking and clinking glasses hit us like a tsunami.

"The Archipelago Arena!" gasped Winter, recalling Repro's description of the incredible room. We faced a glass wall of water—the oval aquarium—through which we could just make out, beyond it, crowds of people enjoying what looked like an underwater dance party.

"Wow, check out that stingray!" said Ryan.

As we ran along the curved length of the coral reef aquarium, trying to find the entrance, I couldn't help but stare up in awe. The stingray Ryan had pointed out was a blue-spotted ribbontail ray, gliding high through the water. Shuffling across the sand was a pair of blue dragon nudibranches, and above them swam a school of blue damselfish. Cobalt blue sea stars hugged the reef, and further along, bluefin trevally, with their iridescent electric blue fins, darted away as a royal blue painted crayfish emerged from a rocky cave.

Only nature could create such mind-blowing color. And only a human could destroy it all.

"Hurry, guys," Cal called out. He ran ahead of us. His white shirt clung wet to his back, and his blond hair flicked water around as he searched for the way in. We ran on, leaving the steward behind with an armful of wet towels.

Time was ticking down.

11:09 pm

We pushed our way past crowds of people and finally ran through the glistening undersea entrance to the arena.

Inside, the atmosphere was electric. The place was crammed with people dancing and partying. Delicate strings of glass balls hung from the ceiling at different heights, sending rainbows of light across the blue room. Cal looked frantically for Mrs. O. and Gabbi, but we had no time to spare. We wormed our way through the crowds to the back of the dance floor towards a stage area.

From the high peak above, within the strings of glass, hung a massive, sapphire-encrusted globe.

I realized Cal was staring at the same thing.

I squinted at it, noticing the edge of something on the top of the sphere. It was hard to tell in the bright blue hue of light, but I was almost positive the object looked mustard-colored. Like the plastic explosives I found in the sculpture at City Hall.

Cal looked at me and nodded. That was where we needed to go.

"How do we get up there?" I asked.

The four of us blinked in the lights and scanned the walls.

"Over there!" said Winter, pointing to a discreet service ladder leading up the wall of the aquarium, near the entrance. "It will take us way up there," she moved her pointed finger above us and squinted, "to that catwalk!"

Sure enough, far above us, a thin maintenance catwalk stretched across the dome and right past the sapphire globe. Winter started snaking her way over to the ladder.

"We can't just start climbing a ladder in the middle of a party," said Ryan. "Everyone will see us!"

"We don't have a choice, we don't have any time to waste!" Winter yelled back.

11:16 pm

People looked up and pointed as we scaled the wall, but they soon returned to drinking and dancing and having fun. I noticed Cal glancing down and searching the crowds for a glimpse of his mum or Gab.

When we reached the steely catwalk, high above the gala, a small, hunched figure over by the top of the blue globe turned and looked our way. An open laptop sat in front of him.

"Elijah?" called out Cal, as we hesitated.

The figure stood up. He was only a kid, but his big dark eyes were intense. Familiar, somehow. I shuddered.

He reached over to the laptop and swiftly tapped at the keys. Graphics flashed over the screen, beeping rapidly. I glanced at the blue globe that hung just below where we were on the catwalk. On top, strapped to it with gray electrical tape, was the rectangular mustard package, beneath the twisted wires and the blinking green digits of a timer.

Cal stepped forward.

The kid closed the laptop and turned to us again. This was the bomber behind the menacing notes? A kid? He smiled, nodding insolently, clutching a cell phone by his side. "Don't come any closer!" he warned. "Or I'll detonate the bomb with this." He held up the phone.

"Why are you doing this?" demanded Cal. "You want *revenge*? You want to blow up this ship and kill my family, along with thousands of innocent people? *Why*? I don't even know you!"

We were all frozen under the unflinching gaze of Elijah's penetrating eyes. He raised one dark eyebrow.

"That's right, you don't know me. Even though we share the same blood, we're complete strangers."

Cal glanced across at me, confused and furious. *The same blood?*

"My mum always told me my dad died a hero," said Elijah, "trying to save a school girl who'd fallen onto the train tracks."

"So?" said Cal, agitated.

"We don't have time for this," Winter whispered.

"But when my mum got sick a couple of years

ago, she finally told me the truth," Elijah said. "That my dad was alive and living in Dolphin Point."

"Dolphin Point?" Winter and Cal repeated.

"Spare us the life story," I spat. I checked my watch. We were running out of time.

Winter was seething. "So you have abandonment issues," she added. "See a shrink."

"Why are you telling us all this?" Cal asked, frustrated. "What's this got to do with me?"

Elijah gritted his teeth and shook with rage as he spoke. "Turns out my father was willing to do whatever it took to make it in life. My mother was afraid of him, and when she found out she was pregnant, she packed her bags and ran and never told anyone where she'd gone. After months of searching, I tracked him down. He was still in Dolphin Point, but his name wasn't the same as my own. He wasn't a Smith. Mum had made that up."

"So?" said Cal. "What was he?"

Elijah laughed wickedly. "He was an Ormond," he said.

Winter looked up at Cal, searching his eyes for understanding. Ryan looked at me, confused. I felt dizzy, the ringing in my ears had returned.

"You're the one who killed my father, Cal," said Elijah. "You're the one who killed Rafe."

11.24 pm

We all stared at each other in shock.

"But Rafe never had a kid!" shouted Cal. "Aunty Klara died years ago!"

"My mother," said Elijah, "didn't die until *last year*. She left Rafe over fourteen years ago. In spite of their many differences, it seems my parents shared something after all—they were both liars."

The sound of Millicent's raspy voice scratched into my head. *There's another one.*

Another one? Another *Rafe*? Is that what my nightmares had really been telling me?

The evil glint in Elijah's dark, terrifying, *familiar* eyes suddenly started making sense. Rafe Ormond's legacy of terror lived on.

Furtively looking around for some kind of weapon, I spotted a heavy wrench lying beside Cal's feet. Without moving, I looked at Cal then directed my eyes towards it. Cal glanced down. In one quick movement, he snatched up the wrench and flung it hard at Elijah's hand.

Elijah shrieked in pain and released his grip on the cell phone. It flew out over the dance-floor and fell into the fish tank with a splash. He watched it as it sank, then he turned back to Cal, scowling.

A surge of fury welled up in me, and I lunged

at him, fists high, when someone suddenly dropped down from above, landing in between us protectively.

The bulky figure stood up and turned to face us.

"You have *got* to be kidding me!" I exclaimed.

It couldn't be. But it was.

Sligo stood before us once more. His pasty skin was a sickly yellow, his body looked lopsided and rotting. His bulging eye was bloodshot and weeping. He was wearing a nurse's uniform, a hospital bracelet wrapped around his wrist.

Elijah smiled from behind him.

"I knew it!" Winter screamed. "You took the other chopper! But the coma? How? How did you escape the secure ward?"

"I have my ways," he snarled. He looked sick. Seriously sick. "Seems not everyone has forgotten about me," he added venomously.

Anger and fear surged through all of us. We had to stop the bomb. We were losing too much time.

I took a running jump and leapt over the catwalk railing, launching myself on top of the globe. I sprawled my body over it as it swung.

"Boges!" Winter shrieked.

The heat radiating from the globe was intense. I hung on, wincing at the pain in my hands.

Cal, Winter and Ryan ran at Sligo, knocking

him to the catwalk floor. Cal and Ryan pinned Sligo down while Winter leapt over them and chased after the fleeing Elijah. She caught him just before he reached the other end of the catwalk and grabbed his arms from behind.

I reached for the bomb, trying to work out a way to disarm it.

Ryan pulled out his phone.

"Don't even bother," said Elijah, squirming under Winter's grip. "I've scrambled the signal."

"It's only four digits!" I called out, still swinging on the sapphire globe. "We only need four digits to disarm the bomb!"

"Tell us the code!" Cal shouted at Sligo.

"Never," he moaned.

Winter pulled Elijah's arms tighter. "Vulkan built this bomb, not me," he said. "I just relocated it. All I know for sure is that it's going off at midnight, and there's nothing you can do to stop it!"

"I told you he was good," Sligo sneered. "Like me, he's determined to kill for what he believes in. This—" said Sligo, shuffling under Cal and Ryan's weight awkwardly and looking around the ship—"was all his idea. Stealing one of my bombs from City Hall . . . and bringing it here . . . *genius*. I just had to be here to watch the beautiful mayhem unfold."

We heard a gasp behind us. A maintenance

worker, alerted to a problem on the catwalk, had interrupted us. Her face was filled with terror and disbelief. She looked at me as I was lying on top of the globe, reaching over the wires of the plastic explosives.

"Bomb!" she shrieked, dropping her toolbox and stumbling as she backed away from us. "There's a bomb on the ship! There's a bomb!"

People on the dance floor below looked up, hearing her cries.

"Bomb!" she continued, screaming over the railings. She reached for her two-way radio, but realized it wasn't working. She threw it to the ground in frustration. "Bomb!" she yelled again. "Bomb! Security! Call security!"

Elijah smirked. "The more the merrier, I always say."

More and more people stopped dancing and looked up. Some people started pointing and shouting. Others started running. In seconds, the place was engulfed in widespread panic, screaming and trampling.

But Cal was distracted by something.

"What is it?" I called out.

He pointed over to the ladder we'd come up.

I watched two small figures—one bigger than the other—in hitched-up dresses making their way up to the catwalk.

Mrs. Ormond and Gabbi.

Cal jumped to his feet, leaving only Ryan to contend with Sligo. The sudden release in pressure allowed Sligo to twist and scramble away.

"No, Cal!" I shouted from the globe.

But it was too late. Sligo stumbled over to Elijah and tore him out of Winter's arms.

"Run, now," Sligo told him. "You must get out of here!"

"But what about you?" asked Elijah.

Sligo shook his head.

Winter grabbed at Sligo's shoulders, trying to pull him back.

I had to get off the globe and help my friends. I twisted my body, trying to get back onto the catwalk.

Sligo grabbed at Winter's throat and lifted her off the ground. He pushed her up on the railing edge and leaned her over.

"Winter!" Cal yelled. He and Ryan burst into a run towards her, but Sligo had already let her go . . .

"Winter!" Cal yelled again, reaching out for her as she began to fall. He caught her right hand. Her other hand held desperately onto Sligo's shirt.

"Help!" Winter cried. "Get me up!"

Sligo teetered over the edge himself. The

shirt tore suddenly, pulling him off balance and leaving Winter hanging onto Cal's hand. Sligo slipped forward, over the railing. His hands caught the edge of the catwalk, and he dangled down, seconds from falling to his death below.

"I've got you," Cal said to Winter. She reached up her other hand for Ryan, carefully avoiding Sligo's swinging body.

Sligo moaned, hanging directly above the edge of the aquarium wall.

Finally, I managed to get off the globe and back onto the catwalk. I dived for Winter, helping the others hoist her back up.

As she swung perilously, the strap on her bag snapped and sent the contents tumbling to the floor below.

"Winter!" shrieked Gabbi, running along the catwalk with Mrs. Ormond. They both fell to their knees, helping us hold onto Winter. "Who's that?" Gabbi pointed at Sligo.

To our left, Elijah was on his knees, holding one of Sligo's hands, trying in vain to help him back up. There was no way he could do it. He was too small.

"Go, Eli," Sligo breathed. His face was red with strain and fear. "Get out of here before this place explodes. You need to get out to a lifeboat . . .

right now. Let me go," Sligo pleaded. "You have to."

"I can't," Elijah cried. "I can't let you go."

"You must," Sligo insisted.

"No! Never!"

And then their hands separated.

Sligo screamed as he fell. His body hit the wall of the aquarium and splashed into the water. He sank fast, like a heavy stone. We watched in horror as a flash of blue and yellow darted out at him from nowhere. Sligo twitched and kicked as he tried to get back up to the surface, but the deadly blue-ringed octopus had found its prey.

Its tentacles lashed out, smothering Sligo's face. He struggled in vain to free himself, but soon the twitching stopped . . . and slowly he sank deeper into the tank, shifting out of sight into the wide, jagged arms of coral.

Elijah pushed past us and ran to the ladder, then disappeared from view.

I tore my eyes away from the tank and looked at Winter, finally back on solid ground with us. She was as white as a ghost. I could see Cal's chest heaving. Ryan's, too. Gab and Mrs. O. looked horrified.

"Ryan," Cal shouted, "get them off the ship! Mum, Gab, go!"

"But I can't leave you and—" Ryan argued.

"You have to get them out of here!"

"But what are you doing?" Mrs. Ormond asked us. "What's going on? We can't leave you!" she cried.

"Mum, I can't explain now. But you both have to get off the ship right now!"

Ryan stood still, fists tensed. I ran back to the bomb.

"Go!" Cal ordered.

Ryan gritted his teeth and nodded. He picked up Gabbi in his arms, and he grabbed Mrs. Ormond by the elbow. He turned and ran away down the catwalk, as fast as he could.

"Cal, no! Boges!" Gab cried. "Winter! Come with us!"

Gabbi and Mrs. Ormond's cries could be heard above all the others as they were taken away.

Cal grabbed Winter's hand and pulled her to him. "Winter," he said, "you have to go, too. Boges will get you to a lifeboat. You have to get out now, both of you. There's not much time."

"I can get myself to a lifeboat, thanks very much," she snapped. She hugged him tight, stretching up on her bare feet. "But there's no way I'm leaving you, and I'm pretty sure Boges won't either."

She glanced over at me, and I nodded. "We're in this together."

"So what do we do?"

"We have to figure out this code."

11:55 pm

I must have tried dozens of four-digit code combinations, but it was useless. The possibilities were just too huge. I was trying to imagine Sligo, planning this bomb for City Hall, and what he might have been thinking when he chose the four digits to arm it.

But the timer just kept on ticking. We had less than five minutes left.

Finally, I looked at my friends.

"It's too late to run now," I admitted.

I rubbed my face with my hands. I was covered in sweat. Winter fell to the floor of the catwalk and thumped it. Cal leaned against the railing and stared, glassy-eyed.

It had all come down to this.

"That's it!" said Winter, sitting up with a jolt. "Down there!" I followed her finger down to the abandoned dance floor below us. She was pointing at a small brown rectangle. She jumped to her feet, ran along the catwalk and dropped down the ladder.

"What is she doing?" Cal asked me. He leaned over the railing again. "Winter, what have you figured out?"

She skidded beneath us, grabbed the book, and was back on her feet in one swift movement. She ran back to the ladder and climbed it like a gibbon.

"When I found this up in the lighthouse," she shouted as she climbed, "there was a page marked with the ribbon. It was a passage from Judges in the Old Testament, chapter sixteen. It's about this guy called Samson seeking revenge on his enemies, the Philistines. That's what Sligo was talking about! Samson was betrayed by a woman who stole his power. Remember how Sligo called me 'little Delilah' back at Coffin Bay? He sees himself as this great hero like Samson, who was chained to huge pillars holding up a palace filled with thousands of people."

Winter clambered onto the catwalk and opened the book, scanning the lines with her finger. "In one final show of strength, he pulled the columns over and brought the palace crashing down on top of his enemies. He destroyed them—crushed them. Just like Sligo wanted to do with City Hall!"

"Hurry!" yelled Cal. "We need numbers! We're down to one minute! What have you got? You need to find the right line, the right verse number!"

"I'm trying!" she cried.

The ticking numbers were flying down in

front of me. "Quick!" I shouted. "We have thirty seconds left before it goes off!"

"Um-ah, um," she stuttered. She flicked manically through the pages.

"Tell me, Winter, please!"

"Here it is! Sixteen-thirty," she yelled. "One, six, three, zero!"

Single digits flashed on the clock. Seconds remained. Cal and Winter held hands and watched on, as my trembling fingers keyed in the numbers . . .

Epilogue

And so Cal was on TV once more, his face broadcast live across the country and the world. We had saved over ten thousand people from dying in an epic explosion at sea. We had saved Mrs. Ormond and Gabbi.

The images of us being reunited with an injured, but overjoyed Repro back on shore were shown over and over again on TV, the Internet, in newspapers, on blogs, on YouTube. Elijah Smith was arrested after he was tracked down adrift on a raft in the sea, surrounded by a ring of civilian vessels.

When a certain Melba Snipe saw the blond boy on her television set again, she smiled. She almost fell over when she recognized one of the other heroes in the background with him. A thin, wiry kind of guy with incredible hands. Shaken and battered on a stretcher, but otherwise in one piece after his rough helicopter landing. Someone she hadn't seen in years. Her son, Albert.

As we sped across the dark water that night, away from the *Sapphire Star*, I took a moment to myself, walking over to the edge of the police boat and peering across the choppy water. I pulled the blanket the paramedics had given me tight against the wind.

"Boges," said Cal, walking up behind me. "How you feeling?"

"Dude," I began. I shook my head and shrugged. "What can I say?"

"It's a tough job being my best mate," he said, with an awkward laugh. "Look, I seriously can't believe I'm doing this again, but I just wanted to say thank you."

Cal paused, looking up at the stars. He exhaled loudly, his eyes shining wet under the moonlight, before he spoke again.

"Thank you for finding me when Sligo had me. Thank you for looking after everything and everyone while I was gone. Thank you for helping me fly the helicopter that got us out here in time. Thanks for . . . for never giving up. You've put your life on hold, your life on the line . . . you've done so much for me."

"Eh, it was nothing," I said, laughing and slugging him in the shoulder. "Everything else can wait," I added, thinking about how I'd go home and convince NASA to give me another shot. Cal shoved my arm down and hugged me. Having him as a best mate had seen me do some wild things in the last two years, things people wouldn't even believe.

But sometimes that's just what a guy has to do.

The police escorted us off the boat and along the length of the pier . . . back to land. A million camera flashes surrounded us. In the flashes, I could see faces I knew—Cal's lawyer, Belinda Quick, his family friend and nurse, Jennifer Smith, the Ormonds' neighbors, Griff Kirby. Mum and Gran were there waiting for me, tears of joy and relief streaking their faces. Everyone had come to see us return safely.

Even Maddy was there, and from the smile on her face, all was immediately understood and forgiven between us.

The police were holding the media back. The press circled like vultures, shouting questions, snapping photos. Amongst them was Ben Willoughby. Cal nodded to the police. "Let him through," he said.

Just before we were fully immersed in the roar of the crowd, I overheard Winter whisper something to Cal.

"It's over," she said. "It is finally over."

And for once, I believed her.

Read them again:

MARCH

CONSPIRACY 365

GABRIELLE LORD

APRIL

CONSPIRACY 365

GABRIELLE LORD

JULY

CONSPIRACY 365

GABRIELLE LORD

AUGUST

CONSPIRACY 365

GABRIELLE LORD

NOVEMBER

CONSPIRACY 365

GABRIELLE LORD

DECEMBER

CONSPIRACY 365

GABRIELLE LORD